THE KILLING HOLIDAY

PRAISE FOR THE KILLING HOLIDAY

The Killing Holiday digs beneath the human psyche and begs the question, what will you do for love? Or better yet, what are you willing to do for revenge? The dark and honest truth comes out in Austin's characters, who become more as the story progresses. The reader is forced to confront their own despicable and basest aspect of humanity: we are all killers—killers of the spirit, of the heart, and of course, the body.

—Rhiannon Marie, author of *SHIFT*

The Killing Holiday will have you hooked, unable to put it down until the whole story unravels itself. Like an epic poet of old, Austin plunges *in media res* straight to the heart of the tale.

I don't wish to give away any of the surprises that lay ahead, but suffice it to say that you'll be presented with a fresh yet familiar tale of love, lust, and death. In lesser hands this tale could easily have drifted into saccharine cliches and overwrought drama, but Austin is a master of her craft and never disappoints. Her characters are multifaceted gems in which we can see fractured reflections of our souls and those we've known, loved, and hated in our own lives, often illustrating how "love" and "hate" are not mutually exclusive feelings.

The Killing Holiday is a must read masterfully told tale by a novelist with the soul of a poet, who leaves us wondering how much of herself was left in the ink on the page.

—John Leys, author of *Whispers of a One-Eyed Raven*

Austin's *The Killing Holiday* takes you to places you wouldn't have expected you'd land as the story weaves one way then another. She does a brilliant job of keeping you in her clutches through to the end when it all finally makes sense.

Or does it? Long after you've read the last page, more than just one question will cross your mind. I'm sure of it.

—Susi Bocks, author of *Every Day I Pause…*

Chills! Continuous chills! I was immediately pulled by all my senses. I adore how deep the characters are. So extremely vivid. Their unapologetic existence melts into my psyche like refreshing, hot cinnamon coffee on a cold, dreary day. Oh, how I love the intensity. I could not put this down. This book sticks like sweet pastry to my fingers, and as the story progresses, burns hot like bullet holes. Afterward, I had to recollect myself. This rollercoaster left me hungry for more of Austin's work. *The Killing Holiday* is a delicious assemblage of madness, love, and endless thrill—not your average cliché, that's for certain. Oh, to be able to write like that... think out a plot the way Kindra M. Austin does.

—S. A. Quinox, author of *Immortalis*

Austin weaves a dark tale of intrigue, love, infidelity, rash decisions, and death in this novella. Her style, as always, is a unique noir, with characters that get under your skin, and a frenetic format that invites the reader into a morbidly fascinating web of lies and deceit.

—Nicholas Gagnier, author of *Eidetica*

"I can never unknow you."

In *The Killing Holiday*, author Kindra M. Austin thrusts readers into a world that is sexy, dangerous, and full of deceit. This is not just a tale about betrayal; this is a book that, at its core, is about love, and "love is madness."
In a cast of femme fatales, dames, and anti-heroes, Austin smashes readers' expectations and brings classic noir into the modern age. Her characters are a direct reflection of our society that invoke feelings of empathy and disgust. What started as a slow burn quickly turned into a fast-paced ride.

Moreover, this neo-noir novella taught me that dark fiction cannot, and will not, wait for permission to be literary vehicles of change. I personally appreciated how this book explores transgressive themes, like sexuality, to create a space of introspection for readers.

—Grace R. Reynolds, author of *Lady of The House*

The Killing Holiday is a disquieting, clever little novel, filled with clement violence, psychological bloodshed, and bitterness wrapped in love. In its essence, *The Killing Holiday* is a love story seeking justice. As a fan of Scandi-Noir I found some of my favorite components at work here—the dark musing, sense of foreboding, and twisted psychology. Reading is a luxury. We want our books to be addictive, compelling and fascinating. *The Killing Holiday* gripped me from the get-go and held on.

This is the second novel I have read by Kindra M. Austin. I can attest, her writing intuitively knows how to keep you hooked. I love a book that I can't put down, and the unraveling of these realistic and mesmeric characters kept me reading until way past bedtime.

—Belinda Roman, PhD., economist, professor, researcher, and author

THE KILLING HOLIDAY

KINDRA M. AUSTIN

HAVERTOWN PENNSYLVANIA

UNITED STATES OF AMERICA

ISBN: 978-1-951724-12-2

Library of Congress Control Number: 2021949039

for the lovers

ACKNOWLEDGMENTS

Thank you to my Indie Blu(e) Publishing family:

Candice Louisa Daquin
Christine E. Ray
Victoria Manzi

I admire you all for your passion and respect for publishing. Thank you for your constant encouragement. Words can never express my gratitude and love for you all.

A special thanks goes to Rhiannon Marie, my real partner in crime. I love you, and I can never unknow you.

PART ONE

2016

1

IT-SPOT

10 October

The room had developed a robust bodily odor. She didn't mind, though, and neither did her lover.

Sound and Color streamed through her earbuds; she lay down on the floor, musing a moment at the smoke rings that rose from her expertly formed lips and disappeared into the ceiling. "Impressive form, wouldn't you say?"

The indifference of his fixed stare was belied by the unending wonder of his gaping mouth. For good or for ill, he'd never been a man capable of holding back his emotions.

She'd been taken by surprise, as well, for the blood spray had been much grander than anticipated; without aiming, she managed to bury the blade deep inside the it-spot of his neck. He landed like a felled tree, and the floor trembled.

Well pleased with herself, she took a final drag of her menthol cigarette, and blew smoke at his perfect face, splashed with crimson death. *Sound and Color* faded out and into *Glycerine*. Her breath hitched at a memory, and she reached for him.

"See?" she whispered, dragging her long left index finger down his cheek. "I fucking told you so."

2

THE AMERICAN

7 October

A newer model taxi parked alongside the pavement, south of the Davies residence, engine idling. From the backseat, a single passenger stared through the windscreen with curious, squinted eyes.

Beatrix Davies leaned into a red car and kissed her darling daughters. "Be good for Nana, and don't eat too many chocolate biscuits."

Nana turned around and winked, and the mousy-haired girls giggled. "We won't mum. We promise," said the elder, and her younger sister nodded.

"Go on, you little liars," Beatrix sighed, though she couldn't help but smile at her daughters. She closed the rear door, and said quite loudly, "I'll miss you." Feeling lonely already, she waved bye-bye until her mother-in-law's Renault turned left at the nearest corner. Nana would surely stop for sweeties, and spoil tea for Camille and Fleur. *She indulges them too much. Just like their father does.*

Starting back to the detached brick house she no longer shared with her husband, Beatrix twitched, heavily anxious. She had noticed the white taxi upon its arrival and knew who lingered in the backseat. She'd invited the visitor, after all. *Oh, well. The time has come. Be brave, now.*

"Thank you. You don't have to wait." The passenger leaned forward and offered the taxi driver a £20 note. He accepted it with a stunned smile, and with no further exchange, he was abruptly left alone to rove the streets for less generous travelers. *Should have given her my card,* he thought.

Beatrix studied the approaching caller from the foyer window, and she didn't wait for a knock before opening the door. "Please, come in. Let me take your coat."

"That's kind of you, but no thanks. I won't be staying long."

"Isn't that your taxi driver passing by?" Beatrix frowned. "He wouldn't wait for you?"

"I didn't ask him to. I've already phoned another service. There's a car waiting for me as we speak. One that hopefully won't smell like vomited beer." The visitor reached into her coat pocket and pulled out an envelope. "This is for whatever it is you have for me. To show my appreciation."

Beatrix nodded, and swiftly procured a generic flash drive from a rather fashionable writing desk. She smiled unhappily. "I've backed up everything I could find that might be useful. I do hope this helps." She extended a trembling right hand, and the two exchanged offerings. "And I'm sorry. I wish we were meeting under different circumstances."

The visitor took Beatrix by the elbow. "Relax, okay? You look like you're about to faint."

"I'm nervous, is all. But I'm doing what's right."

"Are you sure you're not having second thoughts?"

"No," Beatrix said, straightening her blouse. "None at all."

"Good. Because this means everything to me. Thank you. I understand that helping me could cause you a lot of problems. Please, swear to me that you'll take care of yourself and those lovely girls. If things should turn sour for you, don't hesitate to reach out to me."

"I promise, I will." Beatrix opened the door again and escorted her visitor to the pavement. Across the street, a black taxi idled. "Take care of yourself, as well, Ms. Stone. I'm afraid you have no real idea who you're dealing with. He's clever. A master manipulator."

"As clever as I am? We'll see. Again, my thanks."

Oh, well. It's out of my hands, now. But the encounter with the American woman had agitated Beatrix's stomach. She contemplated her own part in the grand scheme over a cup of Yorkshire tea, afraid that her thoughts would grow lungs, and emerge from the shadows, screaming. *Why did I open the door? I could have just changed my mind, after all. He'll never come home, now.* She sobbed inwardly as she opened the thick envelope and fingered the crisp bills tucked inside. In the darkening dining room, Beatrix prayed for clemency.

•••

Ms. Stone lit a cigarette and flipped open her netbook. The flash drive lay on the bed beside her, and she stared at it with hateful eyes. *Now I'll know everything.* She inserted the drive into the port and selected the first file—a video clip. The footage was crisp, and she could nearly smell the sex. She cupped her hands over her mouth and suppressed the woe expanding in her throat.

Two naked bodies writhed against one another in a

noon lit bedroom. The woman kept her face turned towards the camera. "Fuck me harder," she demanded. The man obliged, grunting.

Is he that good? She wondered over the sound of the woman's moaning. *I'd never provoked such enthusiasm.* She focused on the pair of pert breasts, the firm nipples, and slid two left fingers inside herself. *You still do it to me, goddamn you.*

3

BALLERINA & CINNAMON DEVIL

8 October

She met him at Tokyo near Central Station. Tokyo was an intimate, modish bar located on the top floor of an understated building. The weather was lovely for a fading afternoon in October, yet she didn't wait outside for her date. She was incredibly thirsty due to violent nerves. So, Lucas found the ballerina lounging on the terrace beneath a dark blue sky, tipping her second glass of Pinot Noir. The wine was good, fragrant with subtle notes of blueberries, cherries, and French sweet spice.

"Mara Stone," he exhaled, extending his black leather clad arm. "Sorry I'm late. The car park is so crowded, I had to circle until a space freed up."

"I haven't been waiting long." Her voice was wine warm and husky, and the purring friendliness of it startled her. She took Lucas by the forearm, and he helped her up from the taupe settee. Mara quite liked the settee; it resembled a gigantic mushroom.

"You're stunning." And she was—pixie petite with dusky hued skin, and shoulder length hair that shone like black glass. He embraced her, and through hungry nostrils he inhaled the trace of sandalwood and roses; a familiar, amatory scent. "I'm so glad to see you. Vid chats are a pitiful substitute, Lady."

She spoke into his throbbing chest, "Are you going to have a drink with me?"

He pulled away, only slightly at first. "I've already ordered a whiskey and Coke. Excuse me while I fetch it." Lucas kissed her forehead before turning on his heel and heading toward the bar.

Goddamn, you're a handsome cinnamon devil. Mara lit a stout cigarette. The scent of burning mentholated tobacco made her blood sing. Translucent blue tendrils drifted skyward and disappeared into the dimming sunlight. She leaned against the iron rail and watched the devil's reemergence through the rising veil. *Back too soon.*

He moved lithely for a man of his build, for he was tall with tree trunk legs, thick chest, and broad shoulders. Amazing that Adrian had been able to get the better of him. She dragged hard on her cigarette and imagined Lucas with another lover in a dark room, heavy with ardent breathing. *Never yours,* she repeated. *Never yours.* The thought of those two together was nauseating. Suddenly disgusted, Mara smothered the tobacco on the sole of her black satin shoe, then tossed away the filter without even looking to see where it landed.

Lucas observed Mara's nonchalance with amusement. "My darling, would you like a table?" He motioned toward a candlelit corner. Mara nodded, and he guided her by the small of her back. "You look a little green, babe. Is the wine sitting poorly in your stomach?"

"I'll be fine in just a minute. It isn't the wine, it's these cigarettes. I'm used to smoking skinnies."

Lucas raised an eyebrow. *Skinnies?* "Here, let me help you with your coat."

"Yes, thanks." She unknotted the wide belt and allowed him to slip the blue plaid wool down her shoulders. Beneath her coat, Mara was dressed in solid black; chino pants, delicate waistcoat, and a short-sleeved blouse.

Perfection. "I love a woman in black. You're exquisite," he praised while pulling out her chair.

Oh, I know. Mara melted into her seat. "Thank you, Lucas." All of her movements were divinely fluid. She tipped her glass, finishing the wine, then looked up at her date and winked a cocoa eye. Her eyes were lined in black kohl, delicately smudged.

"Another?" With a boyish grin, he regarded her faint rouge lip prints lining the rim of the empty glass.

"I'd rather have what you're having."

"Good girl. I'll be right back." Another kiss on her forehead. His lips were petal soft.

Had the other woman ever appreciated the softness of his lips? Mara wondered, and while she waited, she applauded herself for keeping her shit together. It had been four grim months since they'd seen one another in person. She quickly opened her handbag, pulled out a dull silver compact, and checked her look in the rusted mirror. Yes, she was pleased to see her lip tint was holding up as well as her deception.

Genesis played over unseen speakers; *In Too Deep.* "I've always liked this song," said Lucas, placing a tumbler squarely before Mara. As he walked around the table to take his seat, he brushed a hand over her slight shoulder. "I was happily surprised when you phoned to say you were here on holiday." Lucas supped his drink.

"I needed to get away from it all. It's total madness,

honestly. Adrian has been arrested, despite the attorney his in-laws bought for him. I flew out before hearing whether or not the judge would grant the request for bond."

"Ah. So, he's only just been taken into custody. It's about time, if you ask me. I never did have a good feeling about him."

Mara frowned. "Yes. I found out while I was waiting to board at O'Hare." Her shoulders heaved with a dark sigh.

"What's that look? Don't you think he did it?"

"I don't know. He certainly had a motive or twelve. But he and I grew up together. I know Adrian very well, and I'm more inclined to think it was Ian. Though nothing can be done about that pig of a man now, even if the investigators do find evidence against him."

"And why is that?" Lucas leaned in close, admiring the way the candlelight danced, sun-golden, across the ballerina's features.

"Because Ian's fucking dead. Single gunshot to the head." Mara pressed two fingers against her temple and blew imaginary brains against the brick wall. "The bastard's poor wife found him in their garage. That's what I heard, anyway. There's some speculation over the note he left, though. His wife believes he was also murdered. I'm glad he's dead, for all the grief he put us through."

Christ! Lucas sat bolt upright. *Suicide? Murdered?* He remained silent, considering this Ian Copeland fellow. The two had never met, but each had been well aware of the other.

Mara picked up her tumbler and swirled the whiskey and Coke while she considered Lucas' reaction. "Hey. Are you alright?" she asked before downing the strong drink.

Two empty tumblers called for a swift refill. Lucas had no desire to pause his imbibing. "The wait staff is skiving this evening. I'm sorry, but please excuse me, again."

"Of course."

He came back with four tumblers on a round tray. "I'm sorry you're going through this shit with no one by your side. Tell me, Mara, is it really so dire for you at home?" He looked positively ill.

She snorted. "It's obvious, isn't it, dear heart? I've left my own country, for fuck's sake." She slammed her drink and reached for a fresh one. "Yet, England isn't far enough away."

"Cheers," Lucas agreed, then tossed back the remainder of his own drink in one long, hard swallow.

They were piss drunk within an hour. The pair sang loudly over the speaker volume and cackled at one another's jokes. The other patrons tossed them dirty looks. When the manager of Tokyo kindly asked them to leave, Mara protested with a string of obscenities that made even Lucas blush.

Descending the stairs, he asked, "Jesus, woman, where'd ya learn to swear like that?"

"I just learned how a few minutes ago."

"Liar. You're a liar, Mara Stone."

"So what? All that matters to me at the moment is food. Oh! Let's go into Chinatown."

"Yeah, let's go. They have nice prawn crackers at Palace Garden."

At the bottom of the stairwell, Lucas pushed open the heavy wooden door. They stepped out onto Westgate and headed northwest to Palace Garden over on Stowell. The streets of Newcastle City Centre were hectic, ignited gold and red by hundreds of headlamps and rear lights. A mishmash of techno music blared from various clubs and car radios. The cumulative base was so dense, it rattled rib cages. Mara didn't mind the noise. The ballerina found herself utterly absorbed, as though she was experiencing

Newcastle upon Tyne for the first time. Memories of America had moved to a faraway corner of her mind, liquor soaked and snoozing. She stuffed her small, bare hands into her coat pockets, and welcomed the sobering breeze that stole her breath, bit her nose, and watered her eyes.

It was a fairly brief, and pleasurable walk to Chinatown. The drunkards practically skipped on air, and they laughed the whole way, kicking at pigeons and telling dirty jokes. Upon entering Palace Garden, the evening chill lifted from their bodies and hung overhead for several minutes. Straight away, a hostess offered the prawn crackers Lucas so enjoyed. While waiting for a table, he munched, and Mara watched with keen disgust. The odor was nauseating.

The Palace Garden hadn't changed much since Mara last visited. She observed the too-bright lighting, stained plush blue carpeting, and the low hanging orange paper lanterns, printed with pretty characters that she couldn't read. They were sat at a large, round sticky table nearest the toilets. This was not a restaurant known for romantic ambiance, but the Dim Sum was well worth suffering the noise of flushing water.

"I can call a car when we're ready. Where did you say you were staying?"

Mara's eyes glittered. "I didn't say."

Lucas poured two cups of tea. "I promise, Lady, I've nothing untoward in mind."

She rubbed the rim of her teacup with a long finger, and smirked. "All right, then," she said. "I'm at the Copthorne."

"That's near Pitcher and Piano."

"I know. I love that place."

Lucas grinned. "Care for another drink? I'm in the mood for a gin and tonic."

"Let's get out of here." She pushed aside her cuppa and slinked out of her seat. *Why not? You can't blame me for being curious.*

•••

She hummed along with *Voices Carry* by 'Til Tuesday. The random tune looped inside her head as Lucas exhaled a fusty kind of sweetness against her pulsating swan neck.

"I hope this isn't untoward." Then he sucked her bottom lip, and Mara gasped.

She felt the devil's slick flicking tongue glide into her mouth. It had been ages since she'd felt a feral attraction to a man. His corded arms constricted around her waist. He lifted her, and she instinctively raised her legs, wrapping them around his hips. He carried her to the white down covered bed, and they removed each other's clothes.

The duvet was deluxe, heavily filled. The fabric felt cool against her warm, bare skin. Mara arched her back as Lucas helped her out of her red silk panties. He ran his hands over her dancer's legs; her taut muscles were pronounced and well-formed.

Never in my life have I ever seen legs like these, Lucas marveled. He kissed the delicate skin of both inner thighs, and whispered, "Good gods, Lady." Then he plunged face first into the center of her.

Sweat beaded the length of her thighs. She was nearing her peak. "I want you, Lucas. Now."

He lifted his head and breathed. "Are you gonna mewl for me?" And he licked the liquid salt that dotted her quaking flesh.

She buried her fingers in his mangled hair and tugged, hard. "Please, Lucas. Do it, now."

"Yes," he whispered as he impaled her.

Mara howled with both pleasure and pain.

Their coupling was feverish and quick, though wholly satisfying. Afterward they lay side by side, buzzing. Lucas thought he should go home, but the odor of sex and sweat stained hotel bed sheets made him feel adventurous. Mara was a brilliant adventure he wasn't willing to soon quit. Mara was something special.

"Oh, little ballerina. I'm falling in love with you," the devil declared. But the words fell silent upon sleeping ears.

4

THE BROAD CHARE

9 October

The dimly lit sun penetrated the window dressings. Mara awoke well after the noon hour. Lucas lay breathing deeply. His shock of cinnamon hair against the cloud white pillowcase was quite pretty. She reached out to touch a few rogue strands but withdrew her hand in a snap. She moved from the wrecked bed and went straight to the bathroom. *That will never happen again. I can't allow it.*

She stepped into a steaming shower and wept, wishing she could wash away her indignity and indulgence with complimentary French milled soap. Had Lucas been thinking of his favorite lover in the night? She wondered. Her innards began to constrict, and the memory of a voice she loved seemed to warble from the other side of the hot spray. Mara's mouth suddenly unlatched, and she retched, discarding the contents of her stomach. *Are you watching me? Do I disgust you as much as I disgust myself?*

Mara heard the suite door open and close. She stepped

out of the shower, lightheaded. All she wanted to do was crawl back into bed, alone. "Lucas? Are you still here?" She secured an amenity bathrobe tightly around her waist, and called out again, tiptoeing into the bedroom. She noticed straight away that the curtains had been drawn wide. Grey daylight streamed through the great windows, and a tray of fresh sliced melon, citrus fruits, and washed berries had taken Lucas' place on the bed. A note accompanied the sustenance:

Relax and eat light. We have early reservations at The Broad Chare. I'll pick you up at 3:30, sharp.

Mara threw herself onto the bed. "Goddamn it." She reached for a pillow, pressed it to her face, and screamed. Spilled fruit saturated the sin dirty sheets.

•••

Lucas arrived precisely on time. He was dressed smartly in black motorcycle boots, obscenely pristine, black denim, and a black button-up long-sleeved shirt. He didn't look different from the night before, save the snobbish trench coat he wore in place of his leather fencing jacket.

Mara thought better than to remark on his penchant for dressing darkly. For dinner at The Broad Chare, she chose to wear a long-sleeved navy floral print shift dress, and nude pumps. Her bronzed legs looked delicious.

"You're even more gorgeous than you were last night." Lucas bent and kissed both of Mara's peach blushed cheeks.

"Thank you." Mara took a step backward and considered his clay and moss hued eyes. "You're lovely, too." She couldn't keep the frown from lining her face. *But I wish I didn't think so.*

He flushed, in spite of himself. Not since his last great

16

love had Lucas wanted a woman to see into the pit of him. Perhaps Mara could be the one to hold his heart in her hands, unlike the one who'd held his heart between her canine teeth.

Lucas crossed his arms and considered whether or not he should speak his mind. *Fuck it.* "I know what you must be thinking."

She snorted. "I don't believe you know me so well. But try me."

"You're conflicted. I am, too. I admit that she's on my mind. I know she's on yours, too. How could she not be?"

Holding his stare, Mara said, "So you do know what's bothering me. Bravo." And she saw his eyes go starry. "I'm sorry. I can be a real bitch sometimes. I do know it's been tough, trying to let go of her. I can't even fathom your ability to talk about her. To speak her name."

Lucas sucked a deep breath and exhaled through clenched teeth. He blinked the tears from his eyes. "Listen, babe. I don't mean to make you uncomfortable. Perhaps a line was crossed last night that neither of us was ready for. All I know is that I care for you. So much. I've been falling for you for months now, if I'm being honest."

I can't love you. Mara held up a hand to interrupt, but Lucas raised his voice, stopping her.

"I'm not going to push you. I've learnt my lesson, not to push. I'll follow your lead. After being dumped in such an epic fashion, I'd given up on love. Not that what we have between us is love. I just mean...fuck. I only mean that you're in charge, okay? I'm following your lead."

Mara was no longer surprised by Lucas' gift for softening her resolve but sickened. The ability to maintain her ruse had been a lot easier when they were separated physically by the Atlantic.

"For now, can you just follow me to dinner? I'm

starving.”

Lucas laughed, and then bent to kiss her forehead, “The car’s waiting. Let’s get your coat, Lady.”

In the elevator, Mara mused at how well their hands fit together. *Never yours, never yours,* she chanted inwardly.

The couple kept on holding hands until they arrived at the restaurant. The Broad Chare was a new experience for Mara, and she quite liked the posh pub atmosphere. They ascended the stairs to the dining room and were seated at a solid wood table. Their coats were taken and hung on brass hooks.

“I recommend the rib eye,” Lucas stated, confident. “Unless you are bound to restrictions, being a dancer.”

“After demolishing Dim Sum and saucy duck last night, I think my diet is dead. At least for the duration of my vacation. And anyway, I haven’t danced with a company in years. I can afford to be a little lax once in a while. I teach children, now.” She paused and rolled her eyes. “But I’ve already told you all about the evolution of Mara the Ballerina.”

“Relax, babe. I was only kidding with you.” He laughed and reached for Mara’s hand.

She smiled at him and stroked his thumb with her own. “Let’s eat steak.”

So, Lucas ordered two large plates of dry aged rib eye with watercress, and mashed potatoes on the side. “And we’ll have Strawberry Lambic ale. Keep the drinks coming, will you?”

“I love Lambic ale,” Mara commented.

“So did...” Lucas bit his bottom lip.

“I know. She.” Her heart beat hard against her chest. *My heart, it does bleed.*

“Yes. And she isn’t here. You are. With me.” He stood up from the table in a huff. “Now, if you’ll excuse me a moment, I need the toilet."

"Do what you need to do." *You temperamental twat.*

She watched him walk away. Once he was out of sight, Mara unfolded her linen napkin, then unzipped her handbag. *What the fuck is wrong with me?* She was shaking.

The waiter delivered two tall glasses of ale. He had a brilliant plastic smile. "Can I get you anything else while you wait for your entrees? Some homemade crisps, perhaps?"

"No to the crisps, but I do need something if you don't mind. I seem to be missing a steak knife," she answered while flicking open her compact to check her lipstick. Not a single imperfection looked back at her.

His smile broadened. "You seem to be missing a steak knife? I'm sorry, but how can that be? I set this table myself."

Mara blinked. "I am in fact, missing a knife. I know. It's a mystery to me, as well." She glanced about the table. "Could you bring another one with my meal?"

"Yes." He bent to have a look beneath the table. "I'd be happy to, of course."

"Bring what?" Lucas asked as he approached.

The waiter straightened his back. "Your companion has misplaced her steak knife."

"This is ridiculous." Mara closed her compact with a sharp clack and tossed it into her handbag.

Lucas slid into his seat. "Or perhaps it was a staff error," he stated, equally derisive. "Honestly, man. How does one simply misplace one's cutlery?"

"I haven't a clue." And still smiling, he turned on his heel.

"What the fuck?" Lucas gave a quick shake of his head, then lifted his fragrant glass. He gestured for Mara to do the same.

"To you, Lady. And proceeding slowly." *Clink!* "I'm sorry for my insensitivity. The attitude I gave you was bang out of order. Forgive me?"

"I forgive you. I'm sorry, too."

"Look at you. You're shaking. I promise you, it's already been forgotten."

Mara pressed the glass to her lips and drank deeply. *I will never forget,* she swore to herself.

She lay in bed stuffed with rare rib eye and Lambic ale. Yes, she lay in bed next to the devil, smoking menthol cigarettes even though smoking anywhere inside the hotel was prohibited.

Lucas had fallen asleep naked and perspiring. The cinnamon devil had certainly earned his rest.

Army of Me streamed gently through her earbuds.

"You know you shouldn't be smoking in your room. Especially in bed." His voice was gruff and drowsy.

"Lucas! You scared me." She removed the buds from her ears and dropped her cigarette stub into a clear plastic cup that she'd filled from the bathroom tap. "I thought you were asleep."

He rolled onto his back, and then pushed himself upward into a lounging position, resting his shoulders against the wooden headboard. He flipped on the bedside lamp.

"I was. Until I smelled smoke. Toss me a tab, and I promise not to phone up the night manager." He winked.

She tapped two cigarettes free from the pack. Lucas took one, and he allowed Mara to light it for him. The stainless-steel wick top lighter snapped open with an easy flick of her wrist. He savored the smell of lighter fluid and flint. He smiled at a memory.

Wait. Lucas blinked, utterly stupefied. He'd caught

sight of a familiar inscription:

> *for my violin ~*
> *love, your ballerina.*

"Mara, what are you playing at?"
"I've been dying to show you something. Sit tight."
"Tell me what you're playing at, damn it!"
She smiled, fondling the lighter.
Click. Clack.
Click. Clack.

5

HER ENDING

11 June

Herald was lounging in the grand bay window that overlooked the flower garden when the end came calling. Curled up on the yellow seat cushions amongst a few home and garden magazines, he'd been surveying the backyard through drowsy, golden eyes.

He'd been a keen hunter once, ages ago in his youth. Still, elderly as he was, Herald could sometimes sense a warm-blooded body stirring someplace it oughtn't be, or catch the glimpse of something flitting, and his heart would beat with familiar eagerness. Sometimes he'd consider running out the door and into the wild once again. But then, he'd miss his favorite woman.

On this day, it was a peculiar scent drifting into the kitchen that piqued his attention. He squinted in aversion and noticed the glint of sunbeams bouncing off serrated steel. Herald maneuvered his arthritic body into a crouch and stared wildly through the window screen.

The woman he loved more than any other was outside in the garden, barely three feet away from him, and she smelled of the earth she'd been digging.

Down upon her hands and knees, Rowena was overshadowed by someone strange to Herald. He couldn't comprehend what it was that he was watching. His woman and the caller struggled against one another for just a moment, and then the tang of her escaping blood filled Herald's nostrils. The scent provoked a rumble that emerged from the pit of his chest. His growling went unnoticed, though, and all was still in the garden for an immeasurable space of time.

When at last the backyard darkened, and the bats began to fly, the killer rose up from the rose bed and cried low, "I can never unknow you."

Those hollow words were the last human noises that Herald would hear for two desolate days. And then, the screaming would begin.

6

A FINAL PUNCTUATION

17 June

Adrian spat when he glimpsed Lucas shuffling into the nave. "What's he doing here?"

Mara turned for a confirming glance, and then pressed a resolute hand against Adrian's prickled back. "This isn't the time, Addy. Knock the English son-of-a-bitch on his ass if you want to, but at least wait until after the service."

"It was you, wasn't it? You're the only one who would've told him."

"I'm sorry. I thought he should know. Whether you like it or not, he had the right to be told."

"Why? Because the motherfucker loved my wife?"

"Keep your voice down. We're in church for Christ's sake. And no. I told him because your ex-wife loved him, once. We're here to honor the life of Rowena, after all. This funeral isn't all about you, Addy. I know it hurts, but we need to be grown-ups today, alright?"

"Ex-wife? Our divorce wasn't final, and you know

24

that." He looked at her stiffly. "Who's next? I better not see Ian Copeland here."

Mara considered his tone before answering. "You won't. He was found dead yesterday. Don't you watch the news?"

Adrian grinned. "You're fucking with me."

You have no idea. "I'm not. So wipe the snot from your nose, and act like a man for once."

"You're such a bitch, Mara. I don't know what Rowena saw in you."

"Yes, to you I'm a bitch," she admitted. "And you're a goddamned selfish asshole." Then she took him by the arm and directed him to a front row pew. "We should put aside our differences if we want to get through this. Trust me, will you?"

Adrian raised a thick eyebrow, interested. "I hate your fucking guts. But I do trust you. Always have when it mattered."

"Good." Then she leaned in closer and whispered, "Follow your instincts, Addy. I'll surely follow mine."

"Stop being dramatic, Mara. What's going on inside your head?" She pressed a finger to her pink tinted lips and winked.

•••

Goodbye Baby began streaming on repeat through Mara's earbuds as the first shovelful of dirt was tossed and splayed. The loose earth landed upon the casket with a dead sound—a final punctuation. Mara recoiled at the sight, but Mr. and Mrs. Summers didn't even flinch. Rather, they leaned forward and flashed their spiteful teeth. Yes, their daughter was deceased, but at least she'd had a proper Catholic funeral.

Mara dropped her gaze. Somber Herald stood at her feet, secured by his leash. She'd received some sideways glances when she removed the enormous Maine Coon from her car and walked him through the cemetery.

Goodbye Baby played, and she sang along, soft words dripping from tear wetted lips.

Goodbye Baby played, and she was suddenly watching mourners scatter, tripping over chairs to get away from the horror of Adrian feeding his fists to Lucas. The Englishmen fell hard, leaking metallic scented red from his nose and mouth. He tried to crawl away, but Adrian delivered a final kick before Father Brian finally managed to lodge himself between the men. In a thrilling move, the mighty priest shoved Adrian clear, and then helped Lucas to his feet.

And there in the torn up grass, Mara spied a wick top lighter.

Goodbye Baby played, and Adrian shambled into the arms of Iris and Dane Summers. Lucas stumbled around the cemetery, utterly senseless, and bleeding all over the place.

Goodbye Baby played, and Mara stooped amongst the dying commotion and smoothly claimed the lighter; she ran her thumb over the metal, feeling the worn inscription, then slipped it into her handbag.

Goodbye Baby played as Mara walked back to her car, holding Herald tightly against her chest.

Mara:

You were buried today in the Catholic cemetery outside of town. The shady one overlooking the green river. Our Lady of Perpetual Phonies and Bigots. I had argued to have you cremated, but who the fuck am I? The Corrupter.

Only Aunt Tilly understood us, and she couldn't come to your funeral. She didn't want to witness as your brilliance was hidden from the sun.

I knew what you'd wanted, but you didn't have a will. I watched your parents—studied their ugly faces. They grinned at me when the first shovelful of dirt was dumped on top of your ridiculous casket. You always were a possession to them. Putting you in the ground was their last act of ownership, and they reveled in that shit.

Still. As much as I despise them, I'm glad they weren't the ones who found you.

I'm not as awful as they believe.

I'll never forget the sight of you, dead in the garden. I couldn't look away from your body. The blood, and the bugs crawling all over you. The blackbirds eating you up. My only love, carrion. You were the one person on this earth who knew where I lived and breathed.

I remember our first date—a picnic out at the gravel pits. It was my sixteenth birthday. You kissed me at sunset with sticky lips underneath the pink June sky—my first French kiss. Your tongue tasted like golden wine coolers and cheap menthol cigarettes. You kissed me, and it was the beginning of everything.

But now and forever, it's only me in our bed. The scent of your sandalwood rose shampoo lingers on the pillowcases. I don't know whether I want to press my face into the pillows and scream or take them outside and set the bastards on fire. Set the whole goddamned bed on fire—a funeral pyre for my heart.

I know I won't sleep tonight. I won't sleep any night. Not until I've ended everything.

Adrian:

So, I beat up your boyfriend pretty goddamned good today. I know you'd correct me and say he was your ex-boyfriend. I don't give a fuck what he was to you. He helped ruin my life, and I thought kicking his teeth in would make me feel better. I could have killed him. I wanted to. Still do. Haven't I always said I would kill for you?

Speaking of killing, isn't it hilarious that Mara fucking Stone is just about the only friend I have right now? Cat thief. Herald should have gone to me, not her. You wouldn't believe it, she actually asked if I wanted to stay with her a few days. Screw that. I'll trust the bitch, but I refuse to sleep in the house she shared with you—my wife.

Anyway, I couldn't bring myself to ditch your parents. I'm sleeping on the pull-out in your dad's den tonight. Sober.

Jesus Christ, why am I sober?

Because I'm out of control when I'm drunk. And your Dear Addy has to behave. Person of Interest bullshit. I should never have left Maine, for Christ's sake.

Who knew you'd cause me more trouble dead than alive?

I can hear your mom crying. I haven't cried yet today. I can almost hear you bitching, pissed off because I'm a cold-hearted son-of-a-cunt. Yeah, right. You really had no idea how much I loved you. That's something worth crying about. I loved you the best I could, and you didn't care.

I hope you know that every nasty thing I've ever done to you, you made me do.

You should be in Hell, but I hope not. I hope you're in Heaven, hugging and kissing our daughter.

Damn it. You got what you deserved.

I don't want to love you anymore.

I don't want to talk to you anymore.

Lucas:

You were buried today, and I watched. The love of my life…put in the ground. Never thought I'd see the day. I wouldn't have, had Mara not phoned me with news of your funeral.

I wonder what you'd think of the pounding I received. There was still dirt to be dumped all over you, but Adrian couldn't wait to get his hands on me. Had that bear of a priest not stepped in, I might have joined you, for fuck's sake. Would you have greeted me like you used to do, with open legs? You always did have the propensity to buck propriety.

Mara is the only one who showed any concern for my welfare, albeit in a phone call. Just hung up with her, actually. She apologized for snubbing me at the service, and I get it. I really do. She's a darling, that one. I can also understand why you loved her so. Maybe something beautiful can be forged from your death.

I do hope.

I miss you, Lady. Fuck! I've been missing you since the day you tore my heart out. A part of me will always miss you. But I want you to know I'm not angry with you anymore. And Mara, I realize now that she's an innocent, like me. That poor woman played no part in our demise. She's just another hapless soul who found herself tangled up in you.

What's it like to wield such power? I had plenty of opportunities to ask, and I wish I had asked, just to watch your pretty mouth contort.

Jesus Christ. I hate myself for loving you, still. And I don't know if I wish you were in Heaven or Hell. Does either exist?

Who the fuck really knows? Maybe I'll get you back in another life. I'd never turn you down, babe. I'll go through this over and over again, gods willing, no matter how many times you have to die.

7

IN THE FLESH

1 January

Rowena turned right into the motel parking lot, and just like one of the cool kids she flicked her dead cigarette out the cracked open window with expert fingers. As she drove around back, she looked into the rear view mirror and watched the brown stained filter roll for a spell, then bump to a stop against the low edge of the aged grey sidewalk. The building itself was aged, one of those bargain establishments too close to the airport. She was sure she could stand upon the roof and reach up and graze the belly of a plane with her fingertips as it passed overhead.

The noise will take some getting used to.

She was looking for lucky door number 17. Behind it the Lady would find her prize. She scanned the emerald painted doors through dark shades, as if embarrassed to be there, and the sunglasses actually made a credible disguise. Rightly so, sweet Rowena should have been ashamed of herself.

Shame couldn't have stopped her though, because she was in love, and terrifically selfish. Number 17 was about halfway down the line. She found it and tossed away her sunglasses; they bounced off the passenger seat and landed on the floor mat, accusatory lenses staring up at her darkly.

Lucas watched Rowena back her black Monte Carlo into a first row parking space. "There's my girl. Rowena Fanning, in the flesh," he said to no one but himself.

Rowena didn't notice his figure there in the single window, as she was busy checking her look in the visor mirror. She'd quickly begun to feel sick with bad nerves. Her brain shouted at her. *What the hell are you doing? He could be a killer!*

She laughed at herself then, and said aloud, "Long goddamned way to come, and a fuck ton of money spent just to kill me."

She closed the mirror and flipped up the visor. That's when she saw him through the rear view, standing in the doorway. He was broad and tall with chaotic cinnamon stick colored hair. He leaned against the wide open door, looking out at the parking lot with a rapacious sort of smile.

What the hell are you doing? Ignoring the question again, she gathered up her purse and duffel bag, then took a deep breath. She exhaled three bursts of anxious air before opening the car door. *What am I doing? Going to meet my destiny.*

Lucas stood stock still, taking in the approaching sight of her. She was wickedly gorgeous in well-fitted, faded jeans and tall black suede boots. The early morning winter sun reflected off her hair, blushing yellow light. And good goddamn, those eyes of hers, fiery ice.

Her rosebud mouth smiled, and he felt his shoulder slip

against the shiny door. Rowena noticed, and she didn't pretend not to see; she giggled, and the sound that came out of her mouth reminded her of those conceited kinds of women she'd always detested. Even Lucas knew it was out of character for his Lady to giggle so childishly.

"What the fuck was that?"

They both laughed, equally self-conscious. But the moment passed quickly enough, and he seized Rowena, hugging her tightly and lifting her off the ground.

"Hi, baby. Oh, I can't believe I'm touching you right now," Rowena's voice, oddly soft and coarse both at once licked his ear. "You smell so good."

She inhaled the warm and subtle citrusy scent of him. Her mouth pressed against his neck—barely parted lips, flower petal smooth, and light on his skin. He nearly dropped her.

"I'm in big trouble, Lady," Lucas whispered, returning her feet to the ground. "Your beauty is a poison arrow aimed straight at my heart. You're gonna kill me, babe."

Rowena removed her plain gold wedding band and zipped it up inside her coat pocket. It was important to her that he watch her do it.

"It's only me and you, Lucas. No one else." She traced his jawline with a fingertip—a sharp jawline, square and strong. "I love your face." She placed three fingers upon his mouth—a mouth perfectly wide enough for striking smiles. His eyes, although close-set, she liked the best. They were almond shaped beneath thin, straight brows. "Now I can really study your irises. They're stunning. It's like your pupils are little black suns against a burnished olive green sky, and the suns emit flecks of amber and gold. There's burnt sienna, too. Rolling hills of burnt sienna. I could live inside your eyes forever."

Lucas drew Rowena into the room then, and the door

slammed closed. He held her by the waist and steered her toward the bed, stumbling, fumbling with her coat zipper, and kissing her, tasting her honey mouth. That's how Lucas would have put it. He tasted her honey mouth.

Truthfully, Rowena's mouth didn't taste at all like honey, only menthol cigarettes and diet cola. Lucas didn't care. His hard and eager tongue was rolling around with hers! If he had died right then and there, he would have died satisfied. Or nearly satisfied. As close to satisfaction as he had ever come.

Rowena withdrew herself just long enough to remove her coat and boots, and to draw closed the curtains. The dimmed sunlight was still bright enough to throw shadows, and the motel room suddenly felt like the mouth of a hillside cave.

"I told myself I would be a gentleman." But the scorpion was emerging, unfastening Rowena's jeans, pulling them down to her ankles as he melted to his knees. "I can't help myself, Lady. I want you too badly."

He peeled down her strawberry pink panties, brand new for the occasion, and left them to stretch around her firm white calves. He breathed in her scent, and trembled. Rowena tried to lower herself to the bed, but Lucas grabbed her by the hips and held them resolutely. "I like it like this." He tasted her then, and he didn't stop until she was goose-fleshed and quivering.

Rowena couldn't remember a time she'd so enjoyed a man's mouth. She felt obliged to reciprocate, and for once, she actually wanted to do it. "Your turn," she invited.

"No, Lady. Right now I wanna feel you all around me." Lucas pulled off his black t-shirt, unbuckled his belt, and unfastened his jeans, letting them fall to the floor. He stood before his deadly little archer, wearing baby pink boxer briefs. "I told you I was going to wear pink pants!"

Rowena grinned. "I love your fancy pink pants."

"I knew you would." Then his lips were on hers, and as they kissed, Lucas unbuttoned Rowena's blouse with cautious fingers. He just couldn't bring himself to tear the delicate black fabric from her body. Passionate as he was, Lucas had too much respect for fine clothing to behave so crudely.

Stripped, they fell onto the bed. Rowena lay on her back while Lucas straddled her, kissing her swan neck, flicking his tongue over her collar bone. She buried her hands in his thick hair and thought of her husband's soft blond locks curling around her smooth fingertips.

Don't think about Addy, she rebuked silently. And her husband promptly went away so she could roll atop her Englishman with a clear conscience.

Lucas never once thought about his far away wife, had no feelings of sickness or guilt as he moved inside of his other woman. His preferred woman. He held fast to Rowena's hips, pushing and pulling, pushing and pulling until his toes cramped, and he was breathless, dizzy with buzzing gratification. The thunder he felt in his ears, he didn't know whether it was the sound of his thumping heart or the rumble of an airliner low in the sky.

I can die now, he said to himself. He didn't though, which was fortunate because the room had been paid up through the weekend.

Rowena lay beside Lucas, spent, and panting like a heat exhausted dog. "Goddamn, I need a drink."

Lucas laughed. "I see you looking at that bottle of whiskey on the table, there. We should have some breakfast first, yeah?"

She snorted in good humor and poked him in the ribs. "I wasn't talking about the whiskey, you boozer! Come on. Let's go eat."

They dressed and straightened their hair, rinsed the sex from their mouths, and walked next door to a kitschy chain restaurant only found in the States.

"Should I have steak with my eggs for breakfast?"

"You're back in the land of glut. You can have whatever you'd like."

"Don't I know, Lady?" And then he shit all over his charm by running his tongue along the underside of his top lip.

Rowena glanced around the busy dining room, eyeing all of the moms and pops eating runny eggs with biscuits and gravy. "Don't be gross."

Lucas grinned. "I'm sorry. There's a little pervert who lives inside of me."

"Tell your pervert I never want to see him in public again."

"Oh. You're not taking the piss, are you?"

She narrowed her eyes—slits of ice. "Not at all."

His pale, sparsely freckled cheeks flushed brilliant red. "Then I truly am sorry. I would never purposefully insult you, I hope you know."

"I do know. That's why I didn't reach across the table and smack your foul mouth."

He inhaled through clenched teeth, producing a hissing sound. "Lady, you're turning me on with that brassy attitude."

"Let us eat some steak and eggs first."

They ate slowly, and drank several cups of black coffee, quite amused with one another.

Nineties alternative breathed through circular ceiling speakers.

•••

Back inside the cave, the lovers rolled around for the remainder of the morning. Rowena scored the chance to have a better look at Lucas when at last he let her blow him.

After Lucas climaxed, he said, "You're a fucking goddess, baby. You have certainly earned that whiskey." Then he went and turned up the heating so that he and Rowena could lounge on the bed in their pink underwear whilst smoking menthol cigarettes and drinking American whiskey out of tiny plastic cups. It was quite the tawdry scene, and they chuckled at themselves arrogantly as they dressed themselves in their undergarments.

"I hate the word naughty, but that's what we are. We bring out the absolute worst behavior in one another, and I love it. Cheers!"

Rowena exhaled a great stream of smoke. "We're a Class F couple. Cheers!"

"Class F!" Lucas spit, laughing. "I still can't believe I'm in the same room as Rowena Fanning. I mean, I always had a feeling we would meet, but...this seems like a dream. On the flight over, I couldn't sleep, and I refused the meals, I was so nervous. Actually, I was afraid. I kept thinking to myself, I hope she feels for me what I feel for her. And I'm pretty certain you do. I need to hear it from you though. I need to know before I leave in two days that we're in this thing together, because if I'm gonna hurt, I would rather hurt now before I'm in too deep. But fuck. I think I already am in too deep."

"Baby, I am absolutely certain that I love you. I knew long before I'd admitted it to you. And now I know my feelings for you are much more intense than love. The mere thought of hurting you makes me cry. And the thought of you hurting me? That stabs my heart. I require you, Lucas. I fucking require you." Her words made Lucas weep, not because he had a buzz-on, but because he was a man unashamed to emote.

"What are we gonna do, Lady?" He pressed her bare left hand against his flushed cheek a moment, then kissed her ring finger. "What the fuck are we gonna do?"

Rowena turned her head away from Lucas' glassy, thoughtful eyes, and looked into the streaky mirror hanging on the wall in front of them. She studied the reflection of two indecent people sitting on a sin stained bed, hand in hand. The woman Rowena had thought she knew was someone she didn't recognize. She was in love with this man.

"I don't know," she answered as she reached for a cigarette. She flicked the lighter with a sharp snap. "I don't fucking know."

"How about we start with a shower? I'd love to wash your back."

Lucas shouted, pleaded, "Rowena, wake up!"

No response.

"Wake up!"

A terrible scenario played in his head. *Yes, officer, I'm a foreigner, stateside for only a weekend. I flew over the Atlantic just to pursue a physical love affair with a married American woman. So what?*

He shook Rowena by the shoulders. She was dead on her ass, slumped with the tub faucet pressed against her spine. His eyes went glassy. *No, I wasn't angry with her. No, she did not refuse my advances! And I did not kill her! No, I don't have anyone to corroborate my story. We were having an affair, for fuck's sake!*

Lucas opened his hand, and a wide palm smacked Rowena hard against her left cheek.

She was awake. "What happened?" Her vision was

bleary, and she felt like vomiting. She tried to get up onto her knees.

"Thank the gods! Are you prone to fits?" Lucas took hold of Rowena under both of her arms and helped her stand. "Careful! Let me hold you steady for a spell. Are you prone to fits?"

"Fits. Fits?" She shook her spinning head and swayed slightly. "You mean seizures? No." She touched the back of her head, then the small of her back, wincing and sucking air through clenched teeth. "What the hell, Lucas?"

"Baby, you scared me! We were kissing, then you fainted. I saw your eyes roll back, and felt you go limp. I tried to squeeze you tighter, but you slipped through my arms like an eel. You fell backwards, and then landed hard on your arse."

I did what? Rowena pressed her face against Lucas' slick chest. "Jesus Christ."

"Rowena, don't be embarrassed. Honest, I only care that you're all right. Shit, lady, I thought you were dead! I thought for sure I was gonna be hauled away and locked up in a cell."

"Locked up?" She met his eyes. "For what? Killing me?"

He let go of her and laughed. "Yes. I'm not made for jail, babe."

Rowena stepped out of the tub, and asked over her shoulder, "What if you thought you could get away with it?"

Lucas scooped her up to carry her off to bed. "Lady, don't be daft. I could never, never dream of hurting you, let alone take your precious life."

And kissed her.

"Gamma Sagittarii
Orange, brighter than the sun—
The tip of my arrowhead
Vengeful, deadly does glow.
See Delta Sagittarii,
The center of my bow.
See Lambda Sagittarii,
And Epsilon, the brightest—
Northern and Southern parts
Of my magnificent
Weapon, a sure killer.
Chase you 'cross the Heavens
I do, aimed at Antares,
Bleeding Scorpion heart.
I don't mean to do it.
It's written in the stars."

"It's a beautiful poem. Who's the author?"

"I wrote it. It's called Aimed at Antares." She flicked her lighter. *Click, clack! Click, clack!*

"Are you gonna break my heart?"

"Never." *Click, clack! Click, clack!*

"Is that a nervous habit of yours?" He chuckled, and Rowena's cheeks flushed.

"Yeah, I guess so. Right now it is. I've never shared my poetry with anyone until now." *Click, clack!*

"Can I see that? I've never owned a wick lighter, but my dad has an antique brass one handed down from his father. He keeps it on the mantle to collect dust."

Rowena passed him the lighter. "It was a gift. See here, the inscription."

"For my violin," he read aloud, "Love, your ballerina."

"Interesting. I know you're not a dancer. You're the violin?"

"Yes."

"You play violin? Why haven't you mentioned it before?"

"I don't play anymore." Rowena refused to say another word about it.

They lay silent in the unmade bed, bodies wrapped loosely in white terry cloth, and watched rising cigarette smoke rings merge with dusty sunbeams.

•••

"I should call my wife. I told her when I left that I would let her know I made it okay." Lucas sat down on the bed. "I just couldn't be arsed to do it earlier." And he smiled, amused with himself.

Rowena acknowledged him with a brusque nod and continued to apply her makeup. *Fucking Beatrix.*

This situation between Lucas and his wife was vexing—the strange friendship the two maintained, and her keen interest in his mistress. Adrian would never be so gracious as to lend his wife to another man. In fact, she and Lucas would both end up in the ground. She was imagining what she'd look like dead when Lucas' burst of laughter pulled her into focus. She looked away from the mirror. *Beatrix. Fuck off, will you, woman?*

"Uh-huh," Lucas held up a finger, and winked at Rowena. "Bye." He tucked his phone into the front pocket of his jeans.

"Everything good to go?" Rowena asked as she lit a cigarette.

Jesus, Lady, you smoke too much. Lucas opened the door and ushered her out into the sunny chill. "Yeah, all set. Will you be warm enough?"

"I'll be fine. It's actually quite fair for a January day in Michigan."

They walked hand in hand, following the sidewalk out to the main street. The shower incident had sobered them up some, and the fresh air was enjoyable. Rowena let go of her irritation with the faraway missus, and briefly pressed her shoulder against Lucas.

"This is nice," Rowena murmured.

Lucas squeezed her hand. "I want this life, Rowena. I want to be with you, for good. I'll leave Beatrix and marry you."

Rowena frowned. "But what about your children?"

"What about them?" He slipped the cigarette from between her fingers and took a long drag for himself.

"You'd leave them behind?"

Lucas exhaled forcefully. "Oh, gods no!" He paused to consider the stricken look that marked his lady's face. "I want you to move to England. What kind of man do you take me for?"

Rowena laughed, and Lucas allowed the subject to drop away.

They walked along Middlebelt Road in the sideways breezes. A ceaseless parade of roaring planes moved overhead, and they appeared heavy and balloon light both at once.

This is going to end, and it will break my heart, Rowena thought.

•••

The sun was swiftly setting. Shadows converged and blackened. They'd spent the afternoon talking, and drinking, utterly conscious of the countdown. Both of them had a thick whiskey buzz-on, and they desperately craved a nap. But why waste precious time sleeping?

The couple lay on their naked backs, skin to skin,

beneath a haze of smoke and euphoria. Fightstar played boldly in their ears. *Give Me the Sky*, they sang in unison, and Lucas plucked invisible guitar strings attached to his thigh. Rowena watched his face, and knew she'd never seen the look of a man in real love until that holy moment.

She fell asleep first in the dark of early morning with a cold slice of supreme pizza in her lap, and a smile affixed to her lips; she had tried her damnedest to stay awake. When Lucas realized she was sleeping, he killed the music, and finally closed his eyes knowing that he was the cause of her contentment.

8

A MISERABLE COUPLING

2 January

Rowena rolled over to face Lucas, and she answered a phone call from Adrian. "Hey, Addy," she said purposefully loud. "I'm fine." Lucas opened his eyes, and Rowena touched her finger to his lips. "How are things at home? Are you feeding Herald? Yeah, I miss him, too—my special guy."

Lucas moved tentatively from the bed and into the bathroom where he could safely listen to his lover. He prayed to the gods that Adrian couldn't make out the sound of jet engines rumbling above the hotel.

"What the hell, Adrian?" Rowena sat bolt upright. "I've already told you Mara and I are on the outs. I haven't spoken to her in months. Why are you bothering her? Oh." She pressed a left-over cigarette between her lips and lit it, inhaling sharply. "Yes, I'm smoking!" She blew a whistling stream of smoke. "You can choke on it for all—don't talk over me! I don't give a fuck what—yes, goodbye." She thought better of slamming her mobile against the side table. "You can come out, Lucas."

"Jesus, fuck. Rowena, what's his deal?" Lucas looked ridiculous, standing there naked and flaccid, holding a pouch of Colombian roast coffee grounds.

She laughed, her temper quickly diffused. "Oh, my dear Addy was just checking up on me. He wants to know what the hell I'm really up to this weekend." Rowena rolled her eyes, dragging hard on her stale cigarette, killing it. She reached for another but thought better of it.

Lucas tossed away the idea of coffee. *A shot of whiskey would be finer.* "Can I have one of those tabs?"

"Your indecency is offensive, Sir. Do put on your panties first."

"I will not, Lady! I will stand here and smoke with my cock out if I please. Drink?"

"Of course. Two fingers, please. Smoke?"

"Why, yes." And he reclaimed his place on the bed. "Who is Mara, then?"

"Mara, the ballerina. She was my best friend. Is my best friend? I don't know what to call her anymore." Rowena sniffed, incredulous. "It's been four months of silence between us, and she has the nerve to show up at my door demanding to see me. Addy told Mara I was away, and then he interrogated her. Right. As if she knows something he doesn't."

"Have you ever given your husband reason to distrust you?"

Rowena only snorted before finishing off her whiskey. "I have never been unfaithful. Until now," she lied.

"That wasn't my question, darling dearest." With a wink, he poured her another dram, and topped off his own. "This bottle is running dangerously low." He slugged his drink and went for another.

"You want to get piss drunk so early? Fine." She followed suit, swallowing all of it in one shot. "Booze for breakfast, and an early lunch. I'm fucking starving."

"No, let's not get pissed just yet. I fancy a beer. Do you think we could take a drive later and find a place?"

"Absolutely. I know a great beer I think you'll love."

"Excellent, babe. Come on. We'll get dressed and go next door for breakfast. I could use another steak, and some more of that nice coffee."

"You like that diner coffee? You're not quite as posh as you want people to believe." Rowena laughed, and poked Lucas in the ribs.

•••

Rowena's car was a marvel to Lucas. "It's just so fucking big! I'd forgotten how monstrous American vehicles are. Jesus."

Rowena laughed as she maneuvered her monster Monte between lanes. "I have no goddamned clue where I'm going. I'm all turned around. This area is totally foreign to me. Shit! I'm fairly sure I missed our road."

Lucas was unbothered. "This is a kick, watching you drive. Your facial expressions slay me. You're intense. I'm not nearly as comfortable driving. Of course, I didn't apply for my license until age thirty. And I failed the driving test twice."

A guffaw erupted from Rowena's mouth. "Are you taking the piss, Lucas?"

"I love when you use our vernacular. But no. I was all nerves, babe. I don't think I should have passed the third time." And he smiled the snarky smile that never failed to make Rowena feel hot.

"Middlebelt. Here we go." Tires squawked. Horns

honked. Rowena flipped a mighty bird. "Get the hell out of my way!"

"You're so fucking cool, Lady!"

"I'm alright, I suppose. P.S. it's not really my vernacular. It's my dad's."

Tell me, how long has it been since you visited your father's homeland? Ten years?"

"More like twelve. So?"

"So maybe you should plan a holiday soon."

"I do miss England. I could visit my old Auntie Tilda. You'd love her, Lucas."

"You could visit your auntie as often as you'd like, if only you'd leave Adrian and come home with me."

"I can't leave Addy. He'd never let me go."

"How do you know?"

"He's just not that kind of man. I've tried leaving him before. My parents always sent me back home to him. I guess a bad marriage is better than good divorce. They love Adrian for some goddamned reason. I don't know. I guess they simply refuse to see him for the man he really is. Or I should say, the type of man he used to be."

"By the sounds of it, your husband isn't any kind of man at all. The way he treats you, Rowena. I'd treat you better. Hell, I do treat you better. Think it over, babe."

Rowena didn't tell him she'd already been thinking. She didn't want Lucas to know how badly she wanted him. *Why shouldn't I leave Adrian, and move to England where I belong?*

•••

Lucas sat at the pale wooden desk, and Rowena, at the edge of the bed. They were both in low moods, drinking craft beer accented with orange citrus, and coriander.

The moment the brew had first touched Lucas' lips, he was hooked. "Another thing I'm gonna miss at home," he whined as he chucked his second empty bottle into a small bin. It was five o'clock, and growing dim. The radio-alarm clock glared red from the nightstand, mocking him. "I'm homebound in twelve and a half fucking hours."

In the gloaming they stared at one another until all natural light yawned its last and bid them goodnight—a parting jape. Rowena swallowed the last of her beer, and let the dead glass slip from her hand and onto the floor. Just an hour earlier she'd been straddling her man, pink bra strap hanging off one shoulder, and holding aloft a cold Blue Moon, awfully proud of herself.

She turned up the clock radio. Delores O' Riordan lamented *When You're Gone* through the single speaker.

Rowena felt her soul constrict, and guts twist. "I can't take this." She buried her face in the flattened, sweat dampened pillow and screamed.

"How do you think I feel?" Suddenly more angry than morose, Lucas bawled. "How should I feel? I love you, Lady. You're the only one who can take away the pain. But you won't, will you?" Then he stood up and kicked the chair against the door.

Rowena did stir, but she wasn't frightened of him. She rolled onto her back and opened herself to him. "Come here."

And Lucas collapsed into her.

It was a miserable coupling.

9

HEARTS BLED

3 January

Devastation was nigh. Two hearts bled. What a pitiful sight. Imagine parallel trails of iron scented crimson staining the flooring as the lovers navigated the airport terminal, hand gripping hand.

Rowena mutely rehearsed a sendoff while fighting back the acid rising in her esophagus. Lucas blinked, and bit back tears, chewing open his bottom lip. The airport was practically a ghost town, and the calmness only added to their feelings of desolation.

At the top of the escalator, Lucas freed his hand from Rowena's, and placed it at the small of her back, guiding her to a vacant bench. There they sat, looking at the weekend pictures Lucas had snapped with his mobile phone.

Rowena felt a pang in her chest because she hadn't bothered to take any pictures. She couldn't have evidence for Adrian to find, of course.

"I like this one, here, of you in my shades. They suit your face." Then Lucas placed the sunglasses in her lap.

"They do look better on you, baby."

Rowena puckered her lips and leaned in for a kiss. "Thank you. Now I need to give you something."

"Oh, I have something," he smirked. "I took it upon myself to pack your pink panties into my luggage. I'll not wash them. Ever. I'll sleep with them under my pillow." And they both laughed too loudly for the early hours. Their raucous behavior turned a few sleepy heads.

"Lucas, I want you to know that we're in this thing together. I am absolutely in love with you. I want you. Remember what I told you. I require you."

"Do you? Really? Because I'm in too deep, Lady. Please don't let me leave you thinking we have a future together if we don't."

"I'll prove it to you."

"Damn the gods! I don't wanna go home without you." His mouth squirmed in pain.

They held one another and cried until time tore them apart. One last kiss; the dive was bottomless and brief. It was as though she'd blinked and found herself alone. Her flame flickered through security, dejected. The further away he moved, the dimmer he grew. Rowena watched him until he was no more, totally snuffed.

Concrete feet carried her as she wept all the way to the parking garage. She unlocked her car and opened the driver's side door. The scent of his cologne, spiced citrus, clung to the interior. Lucas had made Rowena promise not to drive until she'd stopped crying. But she was never going to stop, so she slid in behind the wheel, and jabbed her key into the ignition switch. *I should have stopped him. I should have...*

•••

Take off. Lucas watched from his reclined window seat as everything below abandoned all detail, lost beneath unforgiving dumpling clouds. He sobbed inwardly, wishing for a stiff drink.

A layover at Dulles International afforded him the opportunity to catch a nap at a Holiday Inn. But Lucas couldn't help but notice the fine looking bar off the lobby, so he spent four of his six free hours imbibing on bourbon, neat.

The bartender pitied Lucas, and he slipped him a few tumblers now and again, on the house.

"So, my friend. Does your lady have a name?" asked the kind man.

"Rowena. Rowena Fanning." Lucas Davies stood up and slugged back the last of his drink. "I'm working on correcting her surname," he added over his shoulder as he stumbled out of the bar and headed toward the elevator. "I'm working on it."

•••

"Rowena Davies." She said the name aloud, speaking over the radio volume as she drove north. The airport was miles away. "Preach, Janis, preach."

Little Girl Blue was a song best heard in a car speeding toward Hell, and with an aching heart. Rowena hit repeat and increased the volume.

"Tell me, Janis. How the fuck did things end up this way?" She slapped her steering wheel, and then lit a cigarette. "Just calm the fuck down," she scolded herself. Her voice rose above the volume of Janis'.

How does a woman find herself naked and drunk, holed up in a shoddy motel room with a sensitive Englishman?

Easily enough.

Rowena was mostly unhappy with her home life, married to a small town man she'd long stopped loving before she and Lucas ever met online. No one in her real life circle knew of this Lucas, or the mutual friend through whom these two fell into a chasm of desperate love.

PART TWO
2015

10

CHATTERBOX

July-September

The whole thing had begun on a moody Saturday morning in July. Rowena was upstairs in her home office, trying to forget the image of Adrian jerking off in their bed. She'd just logged into Chatterbox and uploaded her latest blog entry when she received a private message from a cigar smoking cartoon gorilla. The subject line read: HELLO! I'M NORTHEASTERN'S MATE.

Northeastern, Connor, was Rowena's favorite Chatterboxer. He'd been the first in the community to subscribe to her Pammy blog, and through him she'd earned a large Geordie following. Rowena had often wondered if she and Connor had ever crossed paths as perfect strangers, as she used to travel with her father to Northeast England throughout the summer. And what about Punch Drunk? According to his Chatterbox profile, he lived in North Tyneside. The gorilla profile picture was obnoxious, but her fondness for Connor prompted her to open the message.

If he's a friend of Connor, he must be a good bloke.

Dear Pammy Pamtastico,

Northeastern (who is much more than a pretendy mate of mine) has recently turned me on to your blog. He says you are the only American he's read on this site who knows how to use sarcasm properly. He thinks you're brilliant.

I'm sending this note to tell you I agree with him. Your writing is smart and eloquently profane, Lady. I'm not easily impressed, mind you, so please trust that I am NOT blowing sunshine up your arse. Though I suspect you're not the type of woman who gives a fuck about the sentiments of others anyway. In fact, I would venture to say you're contrary just for the hell of it.

As I'm also a writer, and a bit of a malcontent myself, I thought you might have a look at my blog? I could be bang out of order here, but I think we could become great mates. I look forward to reading your future posts.

Yours sincerely,
Punch Drunk

P.S. Do you believe in astrology? I'm a Scorpio.

•••

Dear Punch Drunk,

Thank you for the kind words. It means a lot to me to connect with my readers. But I do confess that I enjoy pissing people off now and again. Your assessment of me is a fair one.

I'll have to remember to thank Northeastern for introducing you to my work. I adore him, and I admit I'm a little jealous that you're his friend in the real world.

I did find your blog and read several of your posts. I quite like them, especially your dark fiction. Oh, and your opinions about the American and British governments. Your writing is intelligent and scathing; I love your acerbic wit. I would be happy to call you a friend.

Ever yours,
Pammy Pamtastico (Sagittarius. My husband is a Scorpio, like you. As if it really fucking matters.)

•••

Hiya Pam,

I just want to thank you for taking the time to read me. I always receive positive feedback, but the compliments coming from you truly made me blush. You're a fine writer, and you seem to have an Englishness about you. Have you ever been to England? Like Northeastern, I can't believe you're American. No offense intended, of course.

Do you write more than blogs? I've been working on my debut fantasy novel for the past two years. I've only shown it to one person. I don't know why, but I feel that we're kindred spirits, and I would be comfortable sharing it with you. If you'd be interested in reading it, that is.

Anyway, I hope you have a good day over there, wherever it is that you call home in the States. "Talking" with you today has made mine excellent.

Yours,
Punchy

P.S. Sagittarius, eh? It's a shame you're a non-believer. Perhaps I'll have the chance to try to change your mind.

Dear Punchy

I'm the one blushing. It's flattering to be mistaken for English! Honestly, I've always felt I belong in England. Don't get me wrong, I do love America. My level of patriotism would probably surprise you.

I'd be honored to read your manuscript. I enjoy fantasy, though I couldn't write one page of it to save my life. It takes a special pedigree of writer to produce respectable fantasy. I do have a work in progress of my own, but I'm not ready to share any details.

You should know you've made my day most excellent as well.

Pammy P.

•••

She kept telling herself that theirs was just an innocuous relationship between fellow writers. But when Lucas suggested they speak over the phone, she agreed without hesitation. They hadn't even exchanged proper names.

In Michigan, the mid-September weather was cool and fair, but in Northeast England the wind was whipping, and the great grey sky was pissing down rain.

"Hello? This is Pammy, yeah?"

"Yes, I'm here, Punchy. Can you hear me? I can't hear you so well."

"Listen, today hasn't gone as planned."

"Can you get out of the wind?"

"Can you hear me, Pam? Hello? Listen, I'm out at Whitley Bay. The weather here at the coast is absolutely shite, and my mobile is losing signal."

"What did you say? Can't you go indoors somewhere? Or your car?"

"What? Damn. Pammy, I have someone with me this afternoon—it was totally unplanned. She's coming out of the shop now. Perhaps another day then?"

That was all, though it was still enough for Rowena to fall stupidly in love with the guttural tone of his voice. And hers, soft and coarse both at once, had put Lucas over the edge, and kept him awake that night. Her voice pushed him out of bed and dragged him downstairs to the dining room.

He poured a dram of whiskey, then opened his netbook to pour out his pathetic heart.

•••

Pam,

It's a little after 3 a.m. here in the future. I don't even know what I want to say right now.
I'm probably crossing a line for writing to you in the current state I'm in. Believe me, I've tried sleeping, but I can't quiet your voice inside my head long enough to drop off. I just keep rolling from one end of my bed to the other, wondering if you're lying beside your husband, thinking of me.

I hope you're thinking of me, and that's just fucked up, isn't it? Goddamn, Lady. What is this spell you have me under? Are you at all aware of what you're doing to me? You have to be. You're too self-aware.

Punchy

•••

Lady Rowena was indeed awake in bed, pressed against the smooth, cool wall. While Adrian lay snoring, she listened to the autumn rainstorm falling heavy upon the roof shingles. In her mind's eye, she could see the antiquated monastery at Whitley Bay, and the silvery North Sea waves rushing toward the lighthouse and breaking on the forbidding rocks.

She fell asleep that night on the grey and rainy beach with the wet wind blowing, twirling, and tangling her long, loose hair. When she awoke at seven in the morning, Rowena thought she could taste the North Sea spray cleaving to her lips.

"Damn it," she said, waking her husband.

"What?" Adrian asked, yawning.

"Nothing. A bad dream." She shook her head and sniffed, nostrils flaring. "Why haven't you left for work? Did you call in sick?"

"Rowena, it's Sunday," he yawned again.

She turned her face away in repulsion, and muttered, "Son-of-a-bitch."

"Since we're both up, you want to get dressed and go out for breakfast?"

"Wow," she spoke into her pillow. "You're inviting me to Sunday breakfast?"

"Yeah. Why not?"

"I'll go if your mom will be there. I don't feel like being the tag-along."

"Dad's not coming. I cancelled on him yesterday. I figure I can miss one breakfast with my dad to spend time with my wife. Unless you don't want to, I'll call him right now." He reached for his cellphone.

"Can we go to Banan's?"

"I don't know why they don't shut that shithole down. Alright. Get dressed."

•••

Banan's was a local diner on the old boulevard, a cheerless crevice where they served the most decadent pancakes. It was the only restaurant that had survived the re-routing of the highway. Sometimes Rowena missed the days when she waitressed tables at Banan's during spring break—back when Addy was kindhearted and funny. He'd picked her up at night, and she'd change her clothes in the front seat of his old Buick. They'd travel the country roads drinking cheap booze until the sky turned orange-pink, and then fuck under the eyes of the early sun.

Did he ever really love me? Rowena wondered. *Did I love him?*

The couple sat across from one another at a syrup sticky, undressed table, and filled their mouths between polite remarks.

"I like that sweater, Rowena. Blue's always been my favorite color on you."

"Thanks, Addy," she smirked. "It was a gift from you. For our anniversary last year."

"Yeah, I remember." His response was offensively confident—a goddamned lie.

She rolled her eyes as she stuffed her mouth. "Mmhmm."

"Have you talked to Mara lately?"

"Yesterday afternoon. She doesn't like New York. She's thinking of coming home."

Adrian grinned, but his eyes had a sad, glossy veil. "That ought to make you happy. I know you miss her."

"Yeah, I do." Rowena fought the prickles behind her eyes. *Don't cry. Addy can't stand crying.*

Adrian focused on his plate. "It would be nice to see you happy again. God knows I'm not good enough. I haven't been good enough for you for a long time, have I?"

In that moment Rowena considered telling her husband that she wanted a divorce. But why ruin a fine stack of banana walnut pancakes? "Oh, stop it." She reached across the table and wiped a dribble of syrup from the corner of his mouth. "Why don't you just say what you want to say? I know that bringing me here is just a horseshit excuse for you to talk seriously with me."

"Sometimes I forget how well you know me. It doesn't surprise me that I forget. You're barely even a fucking roommate anymore. No, stop looking at me like I don't know what the fuck I'm talking about. And put that lip away. Why do you always cry whenever I try to have a conversation with you?"

"Addy, calm down. You're causing a scene. I don't know why I even agreed to come to breakfast with you. Consider it a lesson fucking learned."

"You're the one who's crying." He dropped his fork on the table. "Go wait in the truck."

"I'm not finished." Rowena shoved a defiant forkful into her mouth, despite the sudden nausea.

"I'm going to take a piss, and pay the check. Be ready when I get back."

"Yes, Sir," she answered, and snapped a sharp salute.

•••

He opted for the long way home. She was a trapped animal, gagging on the odor of her own anxious breath. *I don't like the expression on his face. This is going to be a big one.*

"Rowena, I've been trying and trying to figure this out. Maybe I'm dense, but you're going to have to tell me. What the hell is wrong with us?" Adrian poked her hard in the arm with his middle finger. "I mean, what is wrong with you? Why are you destroying our marriage? Maybe you don't realize how difficult you are."

His sardonic grin was a punch. "Me? Are you fucking serious?"

"Don't play with me. Yes, I mean you." She started laughing then, hysterical, and couldn't stop. Adrian gripped the steering wheel with two sweaty hands and growled, his heart in his throat. "Do you want a drink? I want a drink. Open the glove compartment." Rowena only sat there laughing, so he stretched in front of her, opened the box, and pulled out a half pint of fine Irish whiskey.

"For fuck's sake, I'm all right, you fucking alcoholic." Then she snorted and waved the bottle away from her face.

He took a long drink. "What were you laughing at?"

Rowena drew a deep breath, and exhaled slowly. "I was laughing because I think it's hilarious that you don't know what's wrong with us. Maybe you should spend some time reflecting on yourself—on your behaviors. Going out with your asshole friends and getting drunk almost every night. Wrecking cars. Jesus, our backyard looks like a junkyard. You're really dim, you know that?"

"What about you? You do some pretty stupid shit, too. I don't like you sitting in your office, playing around on that fucking computer, pretending to be someone else. Talking to God knows who. The radio show is bullshit, but you act like it's a real job. You never want to spend any time with me. That's why I go out all the time. At least the women at the clubs show me goddamn attention. Treat me like a man. I could have anyone of them sucking my dick out in the parking lot."

"Oh, you probably have."

"Maybe." Adrian tipped the bottle and poured a generous slug down his throat.

"You know what? Fuck you, Addy. We used to do everything together before—" and she banged her small fist against the window. *Thud! Thud-thud!* "Pull over. I want out."

"Goddamn it. Don't bang your fist at me. You changed, too. You changed first!"

He made a violent right into their driveway, and the front end of the truck smacked into the garage door. Rowena was pitched forward, and her forehead knocked against the dashboard. She bit into her bottom lip. The tang of gushing blood sickened her.

"You asshole. I hate you." Blood ran down her chin. "Driving like a fucking maniac. You're the reason—I can't look at you right now."

"Oh, damn it." Adrian reached for her head. "You're going to have a bump. I'm sorry. I'm so sorry."

But Rowena wouldn't listen. She unbuckled her seat belt and left Adrian to get drunk in the truck all by himself. She went inside the house, ran to the bathroom, and put her head in the toilet. *Goodbye pancakes.*

11

LOVE IS MADNESS

October-December

Dear Punchy,

I'm sorry I've been silent these past few days. Between the stress of work, and the horrible fight I recently had with my husband, I've not been in the chatting mood. I don't even know why I'm writing you now...I'm feeling lonely, I guess. Maybe I want you to answer, and make me forget, if only for a few moments, that I feel trapped here in this house. In this life. Or maybe I feel I'm safe to tell you things, being so far away from you.

My husband is a maniac. He was driving us home from breakfast the other day, and he laid into me, blaming me for the piss poor state of our marriage. I am not at fault. He is. Everything changed between us after I lost our baby girl. After *he* caused me to lose her. I don't like talking about it. Maybe because everyone in my life said I *had* to talk about it. It's been seven years, and I still won't. It's my pain, and I don't want to heal. The pain is all I have left, the only thing that proves she was real.

Anyway, the other day...he was screaming at me, and when he turned into our driveway, he slammed the front end of the truck into our garage. My head smacked the dashboard. He's been very apologetic. He can barely look at me, though. I have one hell of a black and blue lump above my right eyebrow. It's a good thing my work is in radio—ha-ha! That's not funny, I know.

The plus side of having a crazy person for a husband is that when he fucks up, he tries to make it up to me in the most lavish ways. After all the wine and roses failed, he went out and adopted a cat from the shelter. I'm fairly sure it's a Maine Coon—he's enormous with smoky fur and golden eyes. I've decided to call him Herald. I'm so in love with him, and I'm thankful for the peacetime he's brought into our house. Since Herald has been here, my husband spends more nights at home, and he doesn't complain when I retire to my office for a couple of hours each evening.

•••

Rowena stopped typing, and read through the letter. She swore at herself, and hit delete.

"Time for bed." The old cat leapt from his woman's lap, and waited for her in the doorway. Rowena stared past him, focusing her wet eyes on the stairs. "That's where it happened, Herald." Her voice was low. "Addy pushed me." She extended her arm and pointed a trembling finger at the landing. "I wish the fall had killed me, too."

67

•••

It was seven o'clock on a Thursday evening when Adrian broke the peace.

Rowena had prepared a beautiful lamb stew, and opened a bottle of cheap red wine. The table was set, candles lit. "Fuck it, Herald. Why do I keep making an effort when I don't even want it to work out?"

She stood at the stove, picked out bits of lamb from the pot, and tossed them to her precious. She doted on him so. Between bites, Herald expressed his thanks with a funny sounding meow. Or maybe he was just talking shit about Adrian.

"I don't know. Should I call your daddy? Maybe he has a good reason for being an hour late." So she sat down at the table, poured herself a full glass of wine, and dialed.

"You got 'im!" He always answered, *you got 'im* when he was drunk.

She gulped her wine. "If that were true, he'd be having dinner with me right now."

"What the hell are you talking about?"

"Are you fucking kidding me? Are you at the bar? I hear laughing and carrying on. Who's with you?"

"No, I'm not at the bar. I'm in the truck with Jake and Bill."

"Who the hell is Bill? Can you turn the music down, for fuck's sake? Adrian. Hello?" She lit a cigarette and exhaled furiously.

"Listen, we're going out to Aaron's barn to have a few beers with him. He put in a new wood burner and we're going to check it out. Is that a problem?"

"Yes, it's a problem. I made lamb stew. You love lamb stew."

"It's not like I've never missed dinner before. Save me

some and I'll eat it when I get home. I should be in by midnight."

"What's today, Adrian?"

"Uh, Thursday."

"Today's our anniversary, asshole."

"Ah! Shit. Shit, honey. I'm sorry."

"If you're sorry, why are you laughing?"

"I'm not laughing at you—Jake, watch what you're doing! Listen, Rowena. I'll make it up to you. I promise."

"Go fuck yourself, Adrian."

"All right, fine. *Be* a bitch."

"He hung up on me, Herald! That motherfucker!" Rowena got up from the table, and ladled out two deep bowls of stew—one for herself, and one for her cat. The rest was devoured by the garbage disposal. The cat was served in Adrian's place at the dining table, though he wasn't allowed a single taste of wine.

"Herald, I have some interesting news."

"Meow."

"It's Mara. You've never met her. Anyway, she sent me an email this morning. She's coming home. Tonight."

"Meow."

"I don't know how I feel about it. I do miss her. I still love her. But when she left for New York, our parting wasn't exactly a well-wishing one."

"Meow."

"You know old man, you're a much nicer dinner companion than your daddy. Oh, well. At least I can go upstairs and work as long as I want to."

After dinner, Rowena grabbed a fresh bottle of wine, and headed up to her office.

•••

My dear Pammy,

I've been thinking of you. What else is new?

I didn't want to publicly compliment your latest profile photo, lest suspicions arise. You know Northeastern already believes I am totally smitten with you. He hasn't said anything specifically to me, but I think if anyone is lovesick, it's him. It's obvious to you, isn't it? It should be, what with the way he fucking bleeds all over your blog posts. He even defends your honour whenever some fuckwit posts mouthy remarks, or questions your intelligence. And you're happy to let him do it! I suppose you're just so used to the attention of men that you don't think about it.

Anyway, I know I shouldn't tell you I think you're beautiful, but I can't help myself. You ARE beautiful, Lady. I get the feeling you aren't told very much by those who really matter to you. Your arse of a husband should be telling you every day.

Yours,
Punchy (Lucas)

P.S. I've finally uploaded a photo of myself, if you want to have a look at me. I don't usually share personal photos with internet friends. Please be kind.

●●●

Was he kidding? Of course she wanted a look.

He was in no way physically similar to the fair and sinewy Connor. Lucas' hair, the color of cinnamon sticks, was styled in a chaotic sort of way that Rowena quite liked. She thought his green olive eyes mottled with amber and gold, were striking, even if they were spaced a little too close together. He wore his pensive expression so perfectly, Rowena believed his brooding must be perpetual.

Heartbreakingly charming.

•••

Dear Lucas,

Your name suits you, and I love it. I'll be rolling it around in my head all day. Lucas...the Atlantic is so cruel.
Pammy P. (Rowena)

P.S. Your eyes have the most beautiful coloring.

P.P.S. For the sake of argument, let's pretend that Northeastern (Connor—yes, I know his name) does have a crush on me. What do you care? And don't tell me you don't. If anything is obvious to me now, it's that you're uptight about my friendship with him because it takes some of my focus away from you. You fear I might prefer him over you.

I will make myself clear right now, and I will only tell you once; I like you so much, it would pain me to cut you out of my life.

But you ARE disposable, and I WILL get rid of you if you continue to play pissy pants baby games, or fishing games with me to gain attention/information. If you need a woman's validation, go sit on your mother's lap.

•••

Oh, Lady Rowena,

Could it be you are the daughter of Hengist, wife of Gwrtheyrn reincarnated? Rowena...it is a stunning name for a stunning woman.
I think I know what you mean about the Atlantic because I feel IT, too—the IT between us. Which is why I must apologise for provoking you. I am, if anything, a self-aware man. I admit that I said what I did out of envy of Connor. He has known you longer than I have, and the admiration you two have developed for one another boils my piss sometimes. I feel like an absolute shit. And that is exactly what I deserve. Christ, woman! You really know how to lash a person!
Please accept my apology, Lady.

Ever yours (gods willing),
Lucas

•••

Lucas,

Please, don't be so dramatic. Of course I forgive you.

I only wish that IT would go away. I find myself missing something I've never known.

Yours,
Rowena

•••

Dearest Rowena,

I've not been entirely honest with you. I have omitted relevant information about myself, and I can't, in good conscience, keep it from you any longer.

I have a wife, and together we have two brilliant little girls; Camille is five, and Fleur is three and a half. I adore my children, but I am not in love with my wife. She depends too heavily on me. She has become an emotional burden.

I wonder now if I ever was in love with Beatrix. I know she only married me because I am what is comfortable. I had resigned myself to a life of marital dullness. Then you came along. You've sparked something in me, Lady. I finally know what it is to want to live! Anyway, I'll understand if you no longer want to be friends. All I can say is now that I know you, I can never unknow you. As certain as I am of the air in my lungs, I'm certain I am in love with you, Lady.

Lucas

•••

Lucas was in love with Rowena? It was a ridiculous notion, but Rowena had known it—felt it from the beginning. On her part, it wasn't as though she'd never felt the tugging of her heartstrings whenever she opened an email from him, or didn't catch herself playing the sound of his voice on a loop inside her head, daydreaming. She daydreamed all of the goddamned time, but that didn't mean she was in love, for Christ's sake.

This is fucking ridiculous. He loves me. Well, I'm not in love with him. What the hell is he doing, saying this shit to me?

Still, Rowena couldn't rebuke Lucas for his love claim. She was always happy to play along with his flirtations; flirtations she believed harmless, only because they were separated by an ocean. What was the likelihood they would ever meet face to face? She could hear him then, calling her a tease, or a bitch, or some other slur they only utter in England.

The only fair and proper conclusion is to politely end our friendship. I can't have another reason to be miserable. Yes, I'm doing what is best for both of us. It's time I straighten up and live a respectable life, for fuck's sake.

But her inbox contained yet another note:

•••

Rowena,

I hope I haven't put you off. I know I'm over the line for telling you I'm in love with you, but before you respond, please just watch the music video I've attached.

This song is one of my favourites, and tonight it speaks for my heart. My heart that beats for only you.

Please give it a fair listen. Please give me a fair chance, Lady.

Yours (?)
Lucas

•••

And Rowena was totally undone by a song; one so grotesquely romantic, she watched the video over and over again, falling deeper into the abyss. Her heart retched, and she felt like she was bleeding to death from the inside out.

Just Like Heaven. Son-of-a-bitch. She contemplated her next words.

•••

Dear Lucas,

I'm a bit overwhelmed at the moment. I don't know what to say. I suppose I've known all along. I'll write to you once I've processed it all. For now, I just want you to know I'm not upset with you.

Speak later.

Rowena

•••

Rowena put her monitor to sleep, and stared into the flat black screen for a long, throbbing minute. "I *am* upset." She chugged the remainder of a bottle as she left her office, and stumbled down the narrow staircase.

•••

Rowena was alert when the alarm clock screamed at four

in the morning. She lay still, curled up on her side, pretending to sleep, her face buried in her pillow. Adrian slammed a heavy hand upon the clock, silencing its cries mid-beep. He rolled over and kissed his wife's bare shoulder; she shuddered inside, and he recoiled as though he could actually feel her repulsion.

Then she felt the weight of him lift from the mattress, and she waited for the bedroom light to blaze awake. Adrian always turned on the bedroom light, even though she thought it was a rude thing to do while she was sleeping. Or acting as if she were asleep. The room remained dark though, and Adrian bumbled around buzzing swear words to himself. He thought he was being quiet, but the darkness has a strange way of amplifying sound.

When Adrian left with an armful of clothes, Rowena waited until she heard the spray of his morning shower before she rolled onto her back and pulled down her pajama bottoms. She opened up her legs and used her fingertips desperately, anxiously. It was a wasted attempt to fill in some of her hollowness; when she climaxed, she didn't have to stifle a satisfied moan, but a sob of misery.

Who was Rowena thinking of while she dampened her bed sheets? Certainly not her husband. And not even Lucas. On the other side of town, in a ballerina's apartment, the secret lover slept, ignorant of Rowena's breaking heart. Mara. She was the only one in the world who Rowena had ever fully revealed herself to, and the only one besides Adrian who could never learn about Lucas Davies of Northeast England.

At eight o'clock, Rowena checked her email before leaving for her morning run, hoping to find an empty inbox. But when she did find it empty, she felt her cheeks redden in a flush of nervousness. What if something had happened? An accident? Did Lucas' wife find their email exchanges, or text messages? Perhaps it was only as simple as Lucas realizing his mistake; he was not in love with Rowena after all, and he was too embarrassed to tell her so. She told herself the latter would be a blessing, and the most likely reason for his silence.

Good, she thought. *All for the best.*

Why then, did she feel this sting of rejection so keenly? She dried her eyes, and phoned her ballerina.

"Hello." The sound of Mara's sleepy, sweet morning voice warmed Rowena's cheeks.

"Hi. Did I wake you?" Rowena spoke just as softly.

"Uh-hmmm," she yawned. "What time is it?"

"I'm sorry. It's a quarter after eight. Go back to sleep, and I'll call you later. I'm out for a run, anyway."

"No, Row. I feel like it's been ten fucking years. I've missed you.

"I know. I should have just called you after reading your email. I was nervous."

"Me, too."

"How was your flight in?"

Mara was fully awake now, her voice emphatic. "We didn't land until after one in the morning. It was a bitch of a delay. I ended up taking a nap in the lounge next to a man who smelled like rotten bologna. Bologna! It was awful, Row. The place was overflowing with unwashed bodies, and they all clung to one another."

Rowena huffed and puffed, and she picked up speed. "And rotten bologna, apparently."

"Yes!" They both laughed, long and loud.

"Dinner tonight at my house? I'll cook."

"Don't you want to see my new apartment? I think you'll like it. My mother found a good one!"

"Felicia came through for you, eh? Is it furnished?"

"Somewhat. I don't have a couch or bed yet. I'm in a goddamned sleeping bag. So. Will Adrian be joining us?" Mara did her best to sound indifferent.

"It's Friday. What do you think? Say, around six-thirty? I promise, Mara, I'll come see your apartment soon. Tonight, there's someone I'd like you to meet."

"Can we have steak? I'll bring a bottle of red."

"Sounds good. I do love you, you know."

"And I love you, my violin."

•••

Rowena was at the butcher's, shopping for New York strip when her phone rang. The sudden blast of 80's synth blushed her cheeks and turned her delicate stomach. It was Lucas Davies' designated ringtone.

She took a moment to collect herself before answering. "Hello!"

"Thank the gods you picked up, Lady!"

"Lucas, are you alright?"

"I'm fine. I just wanted to hear your voice, if only for a minute. It's just not the same, listening to you on a loop inside my head."

"I've been thinking about you, too."

Lucas exhaled rather loudly. "That makes my heart smile."

Rowena felt a pebble forming in her throat. "We have a lot to talk about."

"Yes. But these phone calls are bloody expensive. Email me later, yeah?"

"Of course."

"Later then, sweet Rowena." The sound of his throaty goodbye entered her ears and traveled downward, thickly settling into her thumping chest.

78

When she arrived home from shopping, she went straight upstairs to her computer.

Do the right thing, Rowena. Do the right thing for once. You cannot allow this to continue. He has a wife and children, for fuck's sake.

•••

Dear Lucas,

I slept for absolute shit last night. I kept waking up, thinking about what I would say to you today. Please believe I'm not upset with you in any way. Not even for failing to tell me about Beatrix and your children from the start. You don't owe me anything, really. And what do I owe you? There are plenty of things about me I haven't shared with you. I'm not someone who easily trusts; I may appear to be open, but I keep you, like many others, just far enough away from my heart. My blog readers all think they know me; they don't notice the ambiguity—the ambiguity I use like wide open space to keep me safe and free to be me.

You do think you know me, don't you? Lucas, we're just two people connected through words that show up on a computer screen. You say you're in love with me, so you feel our connection is more, I suppose; though I can't fathom how or why you believe you're in love with me.
Not that I don't feel anything for you. I do feel SOMETHING for you. But love? In my experience, people throw the word LOVE around too hastily, even when they don't know what love is—or what it isn't—and when they don't mean it at all.

I do think I should apologize. I've been playful with you, and I'm sorry. I've been told a lot of times in my life that my flirting would get me into trouble one day. Unfortunately, I don't often think about the repercussions of hurting people until the deed has been done, and there's no way of going back. One of my biggest flaws.

This is me being 150% honest with you, Lucas. I respect you and appreciate you as my friend, and as a writer. I adore you in my own way—the only way both of us can afford. Even if I DID love you, neither of us are in a position to do anything about it, are we? Jesus Christ. You have two daughters. I have no desire to break up your family and hurt your children.

I know I can continue our friendship, as I harbor no ill feelings or discomfort. I will understand if you cannot.

Rowena

•••

Mara was half an hour early for dinner. "So that the wine has time to breathe," she explained.

Six months had passed since Rowena last saw her cocoa-eyed lover. *Should I even consider her my lover anymore?* She certainly wanted to, seeing Mara standing in the dimly lit foyer, looking like a beautiful cliché in black leggings and an over-sized boat neck sweater. Rowena flashed a smile, and reached for the bottle of wine, beating back the impulse to sweep away rogue strands of sable hair from Mara's delicate collar bone.

"I'm so happy to see you," Rowena breathed. "Come in!"

"Let's not to do the fucking awkward *should I or shouldn't I?* bullshit." She stood up on her tiptoes and softly kissed Rowena's lips. "There. I feel better now. Don't you?"

Rowena did not feel better. The kiss had made her recognize just how twisted and gross she felt. Too many love interests can do that to a person.

"I do feel much better." And she smiled a flawless liar's smile.

"Meow." Herald had waited long enough to say hello. He rubbed his head against Mara's legs, purring.

"Who is this?" Mara stooped, and she scooped the big boy up into her sinewy arms.

"Mara, Herald. Herald as in *a messenger.* Herald, this is Mara. Isn't he handsome?"

"Yes, he is. Where did he come from?" She rubbed her face against Herald's thick neck as she carried him into the kitchen.

"He was a peace offering."

Mara snorted. "What has dear Addy done now?"

"Same old shit. At least I got a cat out of the fight. If it weren't for Herald, I would have had to celebrate ten wondrous years of marriage all alone."

"Adrian missed your anniversary? That's low, even for him." Mara sat down at the dining table with Herald, and watched Rowena in the kitchen, just as smitten as the first day she'd ever seen her.

Goddamn, she sure can wear a pair of tight jeans, Mara thought. "I'm sorry I came over so casually dressed, Row. I went to an audition at Anne Lily's school of dance and came straight here."

"Anne Lily's? That's quite a drive. I thought you would have gone back to Boyd's Studio."

"I had planned to, but for the sake of curiosity, I went ahead and set up an appointment at Anne's about a month ago. They're offering more money, but I don't know, Row. I miss my kids at Boyd's, and Anne Lily's is more than thirty miles away. I have through the weekend to decide. I'm not going to overthink it."

"A month ago? Are you kidding me?" Rowena turned away from the counter top and looked at Mara, pointing a corkscrew at her. "When we spoke in September, and you said you were thinking about leaving New York, you had already made up your mind to come back. That's why Felicia had time enough to set you up in an apartment. Why weren't you straightforward with me?"

Mara stiffened. "I'm sorry. I just wanted to know how you would react before I arrived home."

"If I hadn't given you the reaction you were hoping for, would you have stayed in New York?"

"Oh, no. I would have come back anyway. I just wouldn't have told you I'd come home."

Rowena poured two exceptionally full glasses of wine, and joined Mara at the table. "This wine doesn't need to breathe." She took a long drink. "Help me understand. You would have moved home without telling me? What? You were going to let me go on believing you were still in New York? What did you think would happen when we bumped into each other?"

"I don't know. Nothing, most likely." She pushed her chair away from the table and Herald leapt from her lap; he landed on the tiled floor with a twenty-two pound *thump*. "I was totally prepared to move on with my life here without you in it. Not that I liked the idea."

"I don't know what I'm supposed to say to you right now. What am I supposed to say?"

Mara reached for her glass, and sipped one, two, three sips. Then she whispered, "Rowena, tell me you love me, and you want to be with me. Say that. Say you love me, and you want me."

Mara was the only person Rowena had ever known who never appeared utterly desperate when she begged.

Rowena fidgeted with her earrings, eyes closed. "You know I love you. I want you in my life, always."

"Here it comes." Mara picked up her glass and drank.

Rowena's eyes snapped open. "Here comes what?"

"The same argument we had at the airport six fucking months ago. The one where I tell you I want you for keeps, all to myself. But you're more concerned with offending your parents and their god than you are with your happiness—my happiness—so you tell me that even if you did leave Adrian, you and I could never be together out in the open. I mean, come on, Row! I don't want to be a secret my entire life. I can't. And it's fucking cruel of you to expect me to be happy enough with being invisible."

Mara stood up then, and she walked out the front door without as much as a backward glance.

What the fuck just happened?

Rowena didn't move or open her mouth in protest, she just sat quietly and let her ballerina go.

"Well, Herald. Looks like you're having a steak dinner tonight."

"Meow."

•••

Rowena spent that night wrapped up in Adrian's sleep heavy arms. Every time she tried to slip out of his hold, he pulled her in tighter. There was a time in her life when simply lying next to Adrian wasn't good enough, a time when she wished she could melt into his skin.

I would ask what's happened to us, but I already know the ugly answer.

In the early hours of the morning, Adrian released her, and as he rolled over onto his side, he said, "I love you, Rowena. I love you more than anything and anyone."

"Do you, Addy?" she asked.

No reply.

I don't believe you. Or maybe this is just the best you can do.

The rising sun lit the bedroom rosy, and Rowena could clearly see her husband's lightly freckled face. She ran her fingers through his hair. She always did love the thickness of his blond locks.

I'm beginning to hate you. I don't want to hate you.

She clutched at her soft abdomen then, and cried for her empty womb. *Even though it's your fucking fault. It's your fault our baby died. Your fault I don't play anymore.*

When she finally slept, she dreamt of a sunny nursery colored lavender and pink. A vacant wooden chair rocked gently, empty in the corner of the room. Rowena's old violin sang softly, *All I Want Is You.*

All I want is you, she mumbled.

•••

Rowena stood in the bedroom doorway and tried to comprehend Herald's betrayal. He was curled up next to Adrian on the couch, napping.

"Whoa. One o'clock. Nice of you to join us," Adrian chuckled.

"Sorry. I didn't fall asleep until after you got out of bed this morning." Rowena yawned, sucking in air that reeked of beer scented flatulence and Colombian dark coffee.

"What do you mean? You were asleep when I went to bed last night."

"No, I wasn't. I was only pretending to be asleep." They looked at one another for a long moment, Rowena leaning against the door frame, and Adrian stroking Herald's giant head. "I want a divorce." *There. I've finally said it.* But did she mean it?

Adrian laughed. It was his cocky laugh, the one that he knew damn well boiled Rowena's piss. "You don't want a divorce. You're just going through another one of your moods."

"Okay, Addy. Why don't you enlighten me? Tell me why I don't want a divorce."

"You love me, and I love you, stupid." His tone was even, and bordered on sincerity.

"You love me? Where were you Thursday night? Oh, that's right. You were out playing with your friends while I shared our anniversary dinner with my cat."

"Grandpa is *our* cat. I like him, too."

"His name is Herald. And he's mine. You gave him to me because you're such a colossal bag of shit."

"Shut up, will you? Damn, Rowena. You never shut up."

"And you will never be able to make me shut up, Adrian."

"This will you shut up," he smirked, pointing to the rise in his plaid flannel pants.

Rowena rolled her eyes.

"One, you disgust me. Two, you're infuriating. Three, Herald is mine. And four, I don't give a good goddamn about your dick."

"Fine. Grandpa is your cat. Now, why don't you get your little ass moving? Do what you need to do to get ready. We'll talk about my dick later."

"Don't dismiss me. I'm not getting ready for shit."

"We're supposed to go to Jake's and play cards. The poker party, remember?"

Rowena started upstairs to her sanctuary. "I'm not

going anywhere with you."

"You have two hours!" His voice shook the walls of her chest.

Rowena closed her office door, then sat at her desk to log onto Chatterbox. Her inbox was full of messages from new Pammy readers. She scrolled past them, looking for anything more interesting, and found several notes from Connor.

•••

Holy balls, Connor. It hasn't been THAT long. What's going on with YOU?

•••

Hey Rowena!

Yay, you're finally here! I've been missing you terribly, THAT is what's going on with me.

You can't just disappear from the internet universe and not tell anyone you're going away.
Screw this typing. Let's vid chat, yeah?

•••

Rowena went to the door and had a quick listen. The shower was running. Good. She tied a piece of red fabric around the outside doorknob, closed the door, and turned the lock. If Adrian came upstairs, he would think she was working.

She returned to her desk, and clicked the green button smiling on the monitor.

"Hiya!"

"Hi, Connor. You look dashing, good sir." He wore a stovepipe hat, ridiculously tall, and a monocle.

"Pajamas, darling?" He scrutinized. "You could have at least dressed for the occasion of speaking with me."

She looked down at her grey flannel pajamas. "Excuse me, I just peeled myself out of bed."

"What's the matter with your face?"

"I slept for shit, that's what!"

"Oh, my poor Rowena." He removed the monocle and leaned into his camera so that she could only see two enormous oceanic eyes. "What's eatin' at ya? Tell your pretendy fiancé all about it."

"It's Mr. Pamtastico. He wants me to go play poker with him at his shit-sucking friend's house."

"I wouldn't wanna do anything with a man who sucks shite."

"I told him I'm not going, but I'll give in. He knows it, and I know it."

"That's not very Pammy like of you."

"Pammy's not real."

Connor backed up some, and he put on his rarely seen serious face; it clashed harshly with his top hat. "She is, though. At least she partly exists. What you need to do is free all of her. Free Pammy!"

"To be Pammy through and through would leave me friendless." She laughed flatly.

"Im-bloody-possible. I would still love you."

Rowena wouldn't have believed Connor could go any paler if she hadn't watched it happen.

"Mind you, now, I'm not in love with you quite as bad as our friend, Lucas."

Rowena straightened her back, and sniffed. "What do you know about Lucas?"

"Please, Rowena! I'm not stupid! Lucas is in love with you, girl. How do you do it?"

"Do what?"

"Make people fall in love with you, of course."

It was a whisper that tickled Rowena's ear, burrowed into her neck and melted down her spine.

"I didn't know—"

"I'm sorry. I've gotta go, my darling. We'll chat later, yeah?"

Rowena could only nod.

Connor raised a hand. "Bye, babe." And he cut the call mid-wave.

Bang, bang!

"Who are you talking to? Are you going to get ready?"

"Adrian, didn't you notice the doorknob?"

"Come on, Rowena! I know you're not working."

"How do you know I'm not?"

Adrian jostled the knob, and the door opened with a moan. He stood stepped into the office and glanced about the room as if looking for something specific. "I think the lock's broken." Then he smiled and added, "Come on, now. Please?" He stuck out his bottom lip, and his eyes twinkled.

Rowena was a sucker for her husband's cute bottom lip, no matter how angry or annoyed she was with him. "Damn it! All right. I'll be down in a minute."

"You'll make the cheesy dip?"

She nodded, "I'll be down in two minutes."

"Nope. You said *a minute*. That's one. So hurry up. I'm done playing around."

When he was gone, she opened the latest email from Lucas.

•••

Dearest Rowena,

I need to speak with you ASAP. It's nothing bad, but still, let me know when we can talk next.

Lucas

•••

Hi, Lucas
I don't want to you think I'm avoiding you. Unfortunately, I can't talk to you at all today. I'll be out with my dear husband until late tonight.

We have a party to attend, and I'm supposed to make dip. I'm sure it will only go to waste. Anyway, I hope you're well, and I promise I'll get back to you as soon as I can. Probably Monday. Forgive me for keeping this email so short.

Rowena

•••

There was no poker game. The guys had been having too much fun burning brush and pouring beer down their throats while they gossiped about the regular sluts at their favorite local bar.

Fucking pigs. Look at Addy, one of the worst of them.

Duke was a vainglorious alpha male, and Adrian didn't like him much. He'd always flirt with Rowena; if smacking her ass and making jokes about taking her out back to give it to her real good qualifies as flirting. Adrian never opened his mouth to defend her honor.

Yes, he'll do.

Rowena proceeded to get shit-faced drunk on full bodied beer, and she bummed mellow blended cigarettes from Duke while they chatted exclusively. When Adrian caught Duke with his hand on the small of Rowena's back, she thought, *show us your balls, dearest Addy*. But Addy wouldn't take them out of his comfortable panties. No, Adrian remained jovial, and only made a failed attempt to wedge himself into the conversation. Rowena accidentally on purpose blew smoke in her husband's face, and then turned her back on him.

I bet Lucas wouldn't let me and another man carry on like this. Even Mara would be in a huff.

Adrian tossed an empty beer bottle into the bin. The high pitched shattering of brown glass silenced the party. "Are you ready to go home, Rowena?"

"It's only what? Eight o'clock?"

"I'm tired. We're going home. Now. Let's go."

"Here's a couple of smokes for the ride home," Duke offered, and he tucked two short cigarettes behind each of Rowena's ears.

"Thanks. Bye guys. Have a good night."

Duke smacked her ass as she walked away. She turned around and gave him a wink.

Adrian was quiet for all of three seconds after Rowena got into the car—long enough for him to back out of the driveway. When they hit the pavement, he shifted into drive, and the squawking tires sounded positively irate.

"What the hell, Rowena?"

She blinked at him, and lit a cigarette. "What?"

"Don't play stupid with me. You're not stupid." He pressed down on the accelerator. "Or maybe you are. You don't know Duke like I do. He's not a nice a guy."

"Oh," she blew smoke out the window, "shut the fuck up, Addy. You and your horny little boy friends can go out to strip clubs, and talk about the hot tits at the strip clubs...you can look at other women and comment on them right in fucking front of me! It doesn't feel too good when some prick is looking at me the way you look at other women, does it? You don't like it when some other prick puts his hands on me the way you do to those cheap-ass bitches at the bar. No, Addy, I'm not stupid, but you sure as shit are. And you're a pussy. Can't even open your mouth to another fucking idiot and tell him to keep his diseased hands off of me. How difficult would it have been for you to tell Duke to go fuck himself?"

"Listen to me, you stupid little bitch—you dumb cunt—you will never turn your back on me again. Do you understand me, Rowena?"

She laughed, and coughed up smoke. "Why didn't you do anything about it?"

"What did you want me to do? Fight the asshole?"

"Yeah. Yeah, I did. I'm your wife, Adrian."

He bypassed a jog, and made a hard left onto a dirt road. "That's not how I do things. I shouldn't have to fight over you."

"Pussy." She pressed harder, and harder. "I'm married to a goddamned hypocritical, alcoholic, pussy."

"Shut your mouth! Listen to me. You turned your back on me. Don't ever do it again."

"I'll do whatever the hell I want. Just like you do."

Adrian slammed down on the brakes, tires spitting loose stone. Dust flew in through the passenger window in a storm cloud. He put the car in park, unbuckled Rowena's seat belt, then reached across her body, and opened the door. There they were—he pulled out his ugly balls and showed them to Rowena in all their glory.

"Do you want to fucking walk home?" His wet lips, acetic, brushed against her ear.

Rowena was shocked, frightened even.

"In fact, I would prefer it. Pussy." She fell out of the car, and kicked dirt. "Go on, you asshole. I hate you! Get the fuck away from me!"

"Good luck walking home! You know what? Don't even bother coming home."

Adrian left her standing on the side of the road, rubbing dust out of her eyes. *I hope he crashes for good.* Rowena let out a sound that was both laughter and a sob as she reached into her front jeans pocket and pulled out her cellphone. The sound traveled over the fields. "Please be awake," she whispered as she dialed numbers.

The phone rang only twice. "Hello! Row, are you alright?"

"Hey, Mara. Adrian and I just had an awful fight, and he's left me out in the fucking country. Can you come get me?"

"Jesus Christ. Your husband is a bastard. How much more are you going to take from him? I would never treat you—"

"I know. Shit. Mara, I'm so sorry for how things ended between us the other night. If you don't want to—"

"Don't worry about that right now. I'm coming to get you."

"Are you sure? I'm such a bitch for calling you this late. I'm horrid."

"Tell me where you are, Rowena. Focus now. I need to know where I can find you."

"I'm dancing around in the middle of Hough Road. Do you have any smokes? I don't have any."

"Yes, Row. Sit tight, I'm on my way. What's your nearest intersection?"

"I don't know," Rowena laughed.

"Damn it. Okay, then. Don't worry, I'll find you."

"Don't take me home, okay? I want to see your apartment. I don't want to go home."

"Whatever you want. I'm in the car, leaving now. Can you do me a favor? Stay out of the road."

"Oh, all right!" But Rowena kept on dancing up the center of Hough, heading north.

The headlights spotted Rowena, and Mara recognized right away that she was impressively drunk. Rowena always swayed and played an invisible violin to silent sleepy music when she was intoxicated. Mara watched her, and she felt her heart sink into her left foot. *Fuck, Row. You could have performed in symphonies if you had gone to Boston. Instead you married Adrian fucking Fanning.*

•••

"Felicia found you a beautiful apartment," Rowena cooed. "Looks like you've been shopping. Nice bed."

It was a studio flat with deeply stained hardwood flooring. An Oriental area rug lay squarely in the center of the room.

"Yeah, sometimes my mother is good for something. Let's get you into the chair." Mara held Rowena's hand and led her to the brown suede recliner, but she wouldn't sit.

"Oh, Mara. A floor to ceiling window. It's huge." Rowena went to the window, and she pressed her forehead against the cool double pane. "I love the river. Don't you? Don't you just love looking at it? What a gorgeous view for my gorgeous ballerina."

Rowena's mouth formed an O, and she exhaled, steaming the glass. She drew a plump heart and added R+M in its center, and Mara pretended not to pay attention.

"I'm still considering curtain options. Do you want to shop around with me?"

"No. I think you should leave your window bare. The view is too lovely to cover up." Rowena turned to face her ballerina and wondered what she was thinking about so intensely.

Mara smiled sadly at the heart that dripped condensation onto the windowsill. "I have leftover take-out from that new Chinese place. Are you hungry?"

"No. Do you have any beer?"

She snorted. "You don't need any more beer, Row."

"Wine, then?"

"Just one glass. I have this homemade stuff my mother gave me as a house-warming gift. I'm warning you, it's pretty potent."

"I hold my own quite well, thank you very much. Look at me. I'm standing perfectly still. And I'm not slurring my speech."

"I know. You've always been a pro," Mara said without a trace of humor. "You really—"

Rowena rushed at her sometimes-lover, slamming her back against the wall. The violin grabbed handfuls of lush black hair and opened a humid, lioness mouth as she inhaled the subtle lavender fragrance. She bent low, pressed her lips against Mara's, and slipped her tongue inside the slick heat. For a moment, Mara thought about pushing Rowena away, but then she felt warm fingers caress her collarbone.

"Do you want me to stop?" Rowena whispered, fingering the waistband of the dancer's jeans.

"No. I've been missing you for too long."

Mara unbuttoned Rowena's blouse, and then their lips found each other once more.

•••

Monday arrived with no word from Rowena. Lucas jammed his phone back into his coat pocket. It was three thirty in the afternoon, which meant in Rowena time, it was still morning. He walked a few paces up the sidewalk in a huff. *Oh, for fuck's sake, I'll send her a text.*

•••

It's me. When you get home, would you be willing to have a video chat? I've set everything up.

•••

Aah, my little archer, you have struck me squarely in the heart. Now, what am I gonna have to do to make you mine?

It was clear to Lucas that Rowena's email regarding her feelings for him had only been a halfhearted attempt to put him off. He knew her kind quite well—that special type of quasi-confident woman who needs to be chased a little bit.

Fine by me, girl. I'll play your game. I'll chase you 'round the moon and sun if that's how it has to be. I've found you, and I will never let you go.

•••

Video chat and voice calls over the computer were new to Lucas, but Rowena was quite an expert, as she was somewhat of an internet talk radio personality. She was picked up initially as a comedy writer by the show's creator and host, who'd been one of her most zealous Pammy P.

95

blog readers.

The more hours in a day that Rowena spent inside the head of her other self, the livelier she felt. The life of Rowena had become damn near insufferable. Pammy P. was shamelessly truthful, and liberal minded. She didn't know the word subservient, which was a problem for Adrian.

Rowena used to wake up at four in the morning every day to pack a nice turkey, or ham and cheese sandwich for her husband before he left for work; per Adrian's request, she would toast the bread, then spread a thick layer of mayonnaise all over both slices before adding the squiggly lines of spicy mustard he liked so much.

But after Rowena began writing under her pseudonym, it wasn't long before she developed a piss poor attitude about getting out of bed three hours early to a pack a lunch she wasn't going to eat. Adrian didn't even eat his nice sandwich most days, as he and his co-workers enjoyed going out for their lunch hour.

"Why don't you get up with me in the morning and pack my lunch anymore?" he'd asked her once.

"What's the goddamn point, Addy? You don't eat the shit half the time. More than half the time. You just let the food sit in your lunch cooler all day, and you bring it home for me to toss into the trash."

"Well, I still need a lunch with me for the days we decide not to go out."

"So pack a lunch. I'm not stopping you."

Adrian's emergency sandwiches weren't as nice as the ones Rowena had always made. She knew they weren't as nice because dear Addy would forget his lunch cooler on the kitchen table every single morning. Pammy Pamtastico didn't give a single fuck about pissy pants husbands and their inabilities to function like adults, so Rowena didn't give a single fuck about Adrian's incapacity to get himself prepared for the day.

Sandwiches are trivial to decent people, and not at all worth getting wrecked over. It really did wreck Adrian. Worse than the lunch situation though, Rowena only went to bed with her husband three nights a week. The other four were online nights, or nights for writing. Four was also the average number of nights Adrian would go out and get totally blotto with his buddies, miss dinner, and stumble into the house a strawberry smoke scented mess at one or two a.m. Precious Addy, he just couldn't stay out of the clubs.

•••

Lucas's problem wasn't the clubs. It was the internet. He kept a room in his parents' home. If Beatrix thought it was off, or if she was ever upset with her husband for having a room outside of their marital house, he was unaware, such was his wife's demureness. And even if Beatrix had taken issue, Lucas wouldn't have cared. He really did require this space away from her sometimes, and it had nothing to do with Rowena.

But how convenient that Lucas should have a secure place to host video chats with the woman he loved. For once, the universe was looking kindly upon him.

At precisely six thirty, Lucas glanced at the time and announced, "Beatrix, I'm off to my mam and dad's."

Beatrix looked up from her book. "What? No tea?" She had prepared a fine chicken curry.

"Have it without me tonight."

She waved him off. "Go on, then."

He went, unaware that his wife, once again, suspected him of improper conduct.

Beatrix wasn't stupid. She didn't have to go searching through her husband's mobile phone messages, or emails to know he was occupied with some other situation more important than his marriage. She read his blog, and she read the comments left by a long haired strawberry blonde girl who called herself Pammy Pamtastico. This Pammy was a pale faced bombshell with sharp, blue tinged eyes.

She, Beatrix, was quite stunning herself, with lengthy russet waves, and dark irises. Rowena surely would have envied the woman's dusky hued features. Beatrix was a pixie little thing, but in the pit of her was a monstrous fire. She would no longer feign ignorance to her husband's infidelity.

•••

Lucas, text me your username so I can find you. I'll call right away, so make sure you have your vid chat up and ready. Can't wait to see you, babe

She found lucas_davies and clicked the green call button. She held her breath.

"Hiya," said Lucas. He smiled, flashing a boyish charm despite the brooding that existed in his eyes.

"Hi." And that's all they said to each other for a long, long moment. It wasn't an awkward kind of stillness, but one of awe, uninhibited.

"Hi," said Lucas again. "Looks like we both fancy black."

"Yes."

"Forgive me, I can't keep from staring. You're so goddamned gorgeous."

Rowena tried, but she could not recall the last time Adrian told her she was gorgeous, and so emphatically.

Look at him. He's nothing like Addy. This man is crazy.

98

He's completely fucking smitten with me.

"Rowena, can you understand me okay?"

"I can. It's so much easier talking face to face. Or monitor to monitor. Our phone call was a disaster."

"It was utter bollocks. Oy!"

"I love your accent. I wish I could pick them up. I think I'd like a French one."

"I like the sound of your voice the way it is. Hearing you talk makes my heart sing."

"You make me feel dreamy." But she only mouthed the words, and Lucas didn't catch the movement of her lips.

"So this is my room at my mam and dad's. My leather divan behind me. Bed there. You can't see it, but I have a flat screen telly. Americans call it the *teevee*. I painted the room myself just last spring."

"Lovely color. It must be quite calming."

"Green is my favorite color. You're right, the sage hue does soothe me."

"I like green the best as well."

"I imagine you're stunning in green, what with your strawberry blonde hair. Is it natural?"

"It is. But my eyes are the wrong color."

"No, milady. Your irises are perfection. When I look at them, I see a thin ring of steel wrapped 'round circles of blue ice. They're not cold eyes, though."

"Lucas, you're entirely different from the men I'm used to."

"What a shame. A lady like you should always be showered with compliments. Men really are beasts."

"I wouldn't call you beasts. Not as a whole. Most of you are just disappointing. Some insipid, others loutish. And almost always unromantic."

"The misconception about us here in England is that we're all downright prudish in the arenas of love, and romance, and sex."

"I would never believe that about you."

"And you shouldn't."

Rowena began to sweat at the nape of her neck. This conversation was headed someplace Rowena knew she shouldn't venture. But her propensity to buck propriety was astounding.

"How do you feel about me, Rowena?"

"You know, Lucas. I feel..."

"You feel what? Please, just say it, Lady." Then he whispered, "Tell me what you feel for me. I have to know."

"This is...what are we doing, Lucas? Do you know? Because I don't. You tell me you're in love with me, and just for good measure, you go on and send me the music video to the most fucking romantic, and tragically beautiful love song I've ever heard in my whole goddamned life. And the way you're looking at me right now, I feel like I'm missing some great part of life I never even knew I wanted."

"Tell me, Rowena. I need to hear you. Say it."

"I feel...damn you. I feel like I love you, too." She spoke the words and like a wicked charm, they both believed her love for him was real.

Quiet. She could only hear brusque wisps of breath through her headset. Then, "Rowena, you have no idea how happy I am to hear you say it." Lucas covered his face with his hands, and his shoulders trembled as he wept. "You have made me so happy, Lady."

"What do we do, now?" asked Rowena. She suddenly felt sick. She wanted to vomit.

I shouldn't have agreed to this video call.

"Good question. I cannot—"

"Oh, no! Adrian is home early!"

"Adrian. Your husband."

"Yes."

Her eyes darted toward the window that overlooked the driveway.

"This is hardly fair." He sighed, and pouted. "Go on, then. I love you."

But Adrian had not come home early. In fact, he didn't even come home on time that night. While his wife spent her lonely hours wondering why she had lied to and cried for a man whom she'd never even touched, Adrian drank at the bar. He bought pretty little ladies named Amber and Tiffany pretty little drinks, yellow and pink.

When he finally did come home, Rowena was so grateful for the interruption of her thoughts about Lucas, she took her husband to bed. But she was numb to his flesh, and once through, she was only left with a terrible ache in her heart, and a dirty taste in her mouth.

"I love you," said Adrian.

"I don't love you, Addy."

"Yes, you do."

Rowena lay awake all night breathing in the acrid air around her, and wondered why men like Adrian never die in car accidents.

•••

Mara sat in her car, parked in Rowena's driveway, and replayed the yummy scenes of the previous Saturday night. *Voices Carry* played on the radio.

Tap-tap-tap!

Mara opened her eyes and rolled down her window. "Hey, there you are."

"Come inside," Rowena invited. "I'll put the kettle on."

Mara was dressed like a dancer, and Rowena could

hardly stand the sight of her.

"I have a late afternoon class today at Boyd's," she said at the kitchen table. She stirred sugar and milk into her tea.

"Excellent!" Rowena sipped her own cuppa. "I'm so glad you decided to go back to Boyd's. I know how much you love it there, and the kids."

"Yeah, I'm glad, too. Boyd's is home to me. And I did want to come home...to everything."

A long sigh escaped from Rowena's mouth. "About Saturday night. I owe you an apology."

"No, you don't. I'm the one who made the decision. I could have stopped you, and I didn't. I kept going even knowing we would both regret it. Row, I am so incredibly, painfully...stupidly in love with you. I have been from the start, and you know I have. You love me, too, and you're afraid of what you would be up against if you did anything about it. I hate you for that, but I can't walk away. We've known each other too many years for me to just walk away. At least not permanently."

"What are you saying, Mara?"

"I'm saying that you won't hear from me for a little while. I'm not giving up on you. I'm giving you some time to reflect. To gain some courage."

Rowena twisted—squirmed in her chair. Sweat began to bead upon her forehead.

"Why would any right-minded person even want someone they've had to fight so hard to win? Really, what is wrong with you, huh? What do I have to do to get you to understand?"

Mara snorted. "I don't fucking know. Why are you such a selfish bitch? You know what? Don't even try to answer. You look ridiculous when you screw your mouth up like that."

For the second time since her return home to East

Hampton, she left Rowena alone in her kitchen, silent and blinking.

•••

Rowena received a text message from Lucas, requesting a video call around three o'clock. She poured a glass of wine, scooped up Herald, and went upstairs to dial her Englishman. She put on the biggest smile she could manage.

"Hey, baby. I hope this is a good time for you. I'm at my parents', as you can see. How are you? You look upset." Lucas looked bright, happy despite the concern in his voice.

Rowena ran her fingers through her long, loose hair, and then sipped her glass; Lucas raised an eyebrow.

"Yes," she sighed, "sangria already."

"Want to talk about it?"

"Right now I just want to look at your face."

"But you're crying, Lady. I can't stand seeing you cry. C'mon now."

"Oh, Lucas, it's just that I've upset a friend...and Adrian. We had a fight—Addy and I—this past Saturday. He kicked me out of the car. In the middle of nowhere. And I had to call someone to pick me up."

"You need to separate from him. I cannot believe the bastard had the audacity to leave you stranded like that. Jesus Christ. How much more of his shit are you going to eat?"

"Please don't yell at me. I won't listen to you yelling."

"I'm sorry, babe. It's just...fuck. I love you, and I'm worried about you. He hasn't put his fuckin' hands on you, has he?"

"Never," Rowena lied. She tossed back her glass,

103

emptying it in three gulps. "I know he's wanted to though, many times." She lit a cigarette and sucked in the poison with gratitude.

"Leave him. Please. It's not like the two of you have children you need to consider."

She straightened her back, and fought off the bile threatening to rise. "You're right. What's keeping me tied to him? I don't love him anymore, let alone like him very much."

Lucas leaned into the camera. "Not a goddamned thing." He smiled and added, "I've something to tell you. I confessed to Beatrix last night."

Rowena coughed out thin wisps of grey smoke. "What? What did you say to her?"

His smile broadened. "We were in bed, back to back like always. I told her I couldn't sleep, that something's been weighing on me. She said she'd already figured it out. She had all kinds of questions about you. I answered them all honestly, and she said you sounded nice."

"You told your wife you're in love with me, and she thinks I sound nice? That's extremely unnerving, Lucas."

"Is it? Beatrix and I are not happy. We pretend for our girls."

"So what now?"

"I can't say just yet. I only wanted to tell you Beatrix knows about us."

Rowena felt her face flush, and she began to sweat. "I don't have the words to explain how I feel about this." She did, though—a long string of obscenities.

"Do you love me?"

"Yes," she breathed.

"I'm so in love with you, too." His eyes began to glisten and drip. "There's lots to think about. And I want to talk to my parents. I'll be back here tomorrow, six-thirty my time. Can we talk then?"

"That's perfect. See you tomorrow."

"Good. Bye, baby. I love you."

"I love you, Lucas."

She clicked the red button, and wept.

"I'm going to Hell, Herald."

"Meow."

•••

Adrian fell into the house totally blotto after midnight, the smell of sweet incense still clinging to his skin and hair. Even in his blurry state of mind, he was amazed that he had managed to drive home without killing anyone. *I need to cut this shit out. Rowena's right to be mad at me. Everything's my fault.*

His wife was curled up in a blanket with Herald, asleep on the couch. He left the bedroom door open, and when he put head to pillow, Adrian peered into the darkness, into the living room and marveled at the woman he loved.

Don't you know I would kill for you? I would. I would. God help a motherfucker who pushes me. God help you, too.

•••

Ian Copeland—enigmatic, charismatic, pragmatic big-brained business fucking piranha—just couldn't achieve the lift off he'd been trying to gain for three years running. When he brought Rowena on board, he was sure his hobby internet radio program would finally attract business partners, and they'd start making a few bucks.

He had always promised Rowena the volunteer gig would turn into a well-paid career. That she didn't earn any money was not the reason she'd decided to resign.

•••

Dear Ian,

This is really difficult for me, and I hope you will be able to appreciate that in time. I want you to know that I have deeply appreciated the opportunity you have given me. Working with you has been a rewarding experience, to say the least. I have grown as a writer, and as a person. Through you, I have gained a friend, so it was through heavy hearted consideration that I've reached the decision to resign. I just can't balance the radio show schedule and my personal life any longer. I'm so sorry. I never intended to leave the show. I love the show, and writing for the blog. It's just all too much for me at the moment.

Please let me know if you'd like some leads on new writers. I've discovered a few I believe would do the show justice.

Ever yours,
Rowena

•••

Ever mine?

That's a good one, Rowena. Radio show a-no-go...so you're leaving me hanging?! I think it has more to do with me not wanting to bring your new English boyfriend aboard. Honey, he is not ORIGINAL. YOU are original. But you're leaving. And I'm supposed to believe you're sorry? Listen, I can find ANOTHER writer if I dig for one. REALLY dig. The trouble will be finding someone who can TALK on the radio. I don't have the time to invest in someone new! But whatever. Thanks for nothing. I hope you fucking choke on your ego. Or better, I hope the next person you screw over puts your lights out...if I don't fucking get to you FIRST.

Ian Motherfucking Copeland

•••

What a scathing response. Perhaps if Rowena hadn't tripped and fallen into bed with Ian once or twice—or seventeen times—he would have accepted Rowena's resignation with some level of civility. Ian Motherfucking Copeland. He was just another broken heart riding the bloody wake of Rowena Fanning.

•••

Dear Rowena,

Beatrix here, Lucas' wife. I do hope you have heard of me by now. Forgive me for my forwardness, but I just had to contact you. I am not ashamed to admit I had to hack into his netbook to find your email address. Before I get into the reason for this email, I must ask that you do not tell Lucas about it. From what I have learned about you, you are not malicious, so I trust you will agree to remain silent. Since Lucas' confession, the two of us have been getting on quite well. Better than ever, actually. He has not mentioned divorce, though I suspect it will come up if you do indeed decide to leave your husband. I'm prepared for it, as I feel our separation has been a long time coming.

That being said, I admit I would prefer to live a phony life with my family all under one roof. But please believe, I am not writing to you to beg you to leave my husband alone because I want to hold on to him. I mean only to give you fair warning. I had been hoping I wouldn't need to, however it is necessary now that Lucas plans to travel to the States to meet you.

You see, you are not the first American woman Lucas has fallen for. There have been others I'm sure about, writers and other artist types that he'd taken a shine to. I don't want to see you end up ruined like the others. Please take care.

Beatrix

•••

Yes, November had been a pretty bleak month for Rowena. Mara was still hidden away silent, and Connor had deleted his Chatterbox account without a word. Adrian suffered from a mad case of baby fever, she'd received a death threat from Ian, and an email from her online boyfriend's wife that had left her feeling quite chilled. The worst though was Thanksgiving dinner at her parents' condo.

"What's the matter, Love?" Rowena's mother asked in the quiet kitchen. "Do you need a pill for your nerves?" She opened the cupboard and searched through a cluster of orange tinted plastic.

"Mom, I'm coming unraveled, and no tiny white tablet can fix me."

She clenched her teeth.

Can't you just hug me?

"What you need is a baby. I was telling Adrian—"

"I knew it! Addy doesn't know I'm taking birth control, and he's been trying to mount me—"

Her mother winced. "Don't be vulgar, dear heart. Just get off that wicked pill and do what you're supposed to do. Give your dad and me our first grandchild. You'll be thirty next month, Rowena. Come on, now."

"I've been thinking about leaving him, Mom."

"Leaving who?"

Rowena sighed. "Addy." Then she looked straight into her mother's muddy river eyes; she said low and stern, "I want a divorce. Your beloved Adrian isn't the man you think you know. He hasn't been the same since the accident. Neither have I, but he's over the edge."

"Does this have anything to do with Mara? I'll bet it does. You have to know that your relationship with her is unhealthy. Inappropriate. Immoral. Are you still carrying on with her that way? My God, Rowena, when your dad caught you together as teens...you said you'd never do that again! You went to confession, and promised never to...do you want to go to Hell?"

"We were eighteen. Adults. Anyway, it isn't Mara. Will you fucking listen to me for once? It's Adrian. He's an alcoholic. He goes out almost every night after work to clubs and flirts with other skanky women. He's left me stranded on the side of the road—"

"I know things have never been easy for you two. I really do. I am a woman after all, and I know how you feel. But the fact is, Rowena, it's your duty to make an effort to please your husband. If you were more pleasing, Adrian would be happy to come home to you. He wouldn't feel like he has to look elsewhere for the attention he deserves. What you need to do is attend mass regularly as a couple. Couples need God to keep them strong."

What I need to do is run away to England. To hell with whatever Beatrix has to say. I don't care. I know Lucas loves me.

Rowena huffed, feeling defeated. "God doesn't have anything for me. I don't want Adrian, okay? We both deserve better than each other."

"That's a terrible thing to say. You make me feel so ashamed sometimes. And what makes it worse is you don't have any siblings to relieve the pain you cause me." She dabbed at her glassy eyes with the corner of her apron.

"I love you, Mom," she mumbled. Then she put a cigarette in her mouth, lit it, and blew a great grey stream of smoke into her mother's face. "I love you even though you're mostly a sad, abhorrent bitch. You make me feel ashamed, too. Here, let me carry out the turkey for you."

Rowena's little family gathered around an oval dining room table laden at the center with typical white American Thanksgiving fare. Hand in hand they recited a prayer of gratitude. The scene looked like a humble holiday greeting card.

A gorgeous lie. A goddamned gorgeous lie.

"What's this, Iris? I was hoping for mushy peas. I flew near thirteen hours to eat with you, and there's no mushy peas? Are mushy peas all that difficult to prepare?"

Tilda was red-nosed, sweet sherry drunk. Good old Aunt Tilly, she was Rowena's favorite among her father's three elder sisters.

Tilda never liked Iris purely because Dane had moved to America and converted to Catholicism after he met and fell hard for the Yankee; Iris had been on holiday in England for the first time. The two met in Newcastle upon Tyne, and from there, they spent a month traveling together, taking their time to reach London, then onward to seaside Portsmouth.

Rowena reached for the bowl of beady peas.

"Would you like me to mush your peas, Aunt Tilly?"

Iris slapped Rowena's hand. "No one is getting up from this table to mush peas. Tilda, I'm sorry, I didn't know mushy peas meant that much to you. Next year, you can have an entire pot of mushy peas all to yourself."

"That's about enough," said Dane, and he took his wife's hand, rubbing her crepe paper skin with his thumb. "Leave poor Iris alone."

"I'm sorry, dear." But Tilda wasn't sorry. She waited for Iris to swallow her first mouthful before she asked, "Pour me another sherry?"

Rowena suppressed a chuckle. "I'll have a bourbon, too. Adrian, bourbon?"

"No, thank you. But you sit, Iris. Let me pour the drinks." He winked at Rowena.

Rowena could never figure out why Adrian bothered so much to impress her parents; he wasn't the slightest bit fond of either of them, the uppity twats.

The more alcohol Rowena downed, the more she thought about her relationship with her father. She missed him painfully; they'd always been close until Dane caught her and Mara performing abominable acts on one another.. What he'd done to Mara that last holiday in England, Rowena could never forgive. It had happened in June 2004, the first time Mara had ever seen magnificent England with her own eyes.

•••

The Most Pretentious Hotel of Newcastle City Centre boasted a grand view of the River Tyne and Millennium Bridge. Rowena had stayed there every trip she'd ever made to England with her father, and she never grew bored of the scenery. Dane had rented the girls a room of

111

their own, provided they did not object to him holding an extra key. Every morning for a month, Mara would rise with the sun, and she'd snap a photo of the rosy orange lit River Tyne from the window.

While Dane tended to business, Rowena and Mara mostly spent their afternoons admiring the Tudor style structures, and wandering in and out of shops—boutiques, book stores, bakeries. For lunch they'd eat sweet and sour chicken or Dim Sum at a great place in Chinatown, or sandwiches at Pret. And they did plenty of day drinking at a chic marbled bar, or inside a shadowy brick tavern with low arched ceilings that once was a wine cellar. A late dinner and a few Japanese beers with Dane at a hibachi grill just outside the buzzing city completed the weekday activities. On Sundays, Dane would drive them all to Whitley Bay in a rental car. Mara would dip her dancer toes into the chill North Sea while Rowena argued with the seagulls, and picked out stones to take back home.

The first Sunday afternoon at the bay, they were served tea at Aunt Tilly's. Tilda and the other aunts adored Mara; *Look at her! She's so small, a doll, like! So exotic.* The succeeding Sundays, Dane ordered take-away fish and chips, and the three filled their faces in the company of tourists snapping pictures of the seaside monastery— sandstone brown and ages old, standing beautifully reverent upon the lawn so green, no words exist that could describe its brilliance.

Rowena promised herself to move home someday.

"Are we not going to see Aunt Tilly and the rest again before we go home?" Mara had asked.

"Dad and Aunt Tilly are at odds. This shit happens every time they see each other. Aunt Tilly is always insulting my mom. It infuriates my dad, but more than that, it hurts his feelings because he loves his sister terribly.

They most likely won't speak again until Aunt Tilly flies over in November."

"What about his other sisters?"

"Dad's never been too close with them. They're so much older, Maggie and Susy were already married and pregnant by the time Tilda was born, then Dad a year later. It makes me sad. Dad only really has Aunt Tilly now. He misses my grandma and grandpa...it breaks my heart whenever I catch him crying over them."

"Aunt Tilly doesn't have many kind words to say about them."

"No. But what of it?"

"Maybe they were assholes."

"Maybe, but that's not for you to decide."

They didn't speak to one another for the rest of the day. Dane noticed the tension between the girls, and he naturally assumed Mara had done something to upset his dear Rowena. Dane had never been fond of Mara, as there was something about her that prickled his skin...the way the doll would steal glances at Rowena, or lightly graze the small of Rowena's back when she thought no one was paying attention.

He was so bothered in fact, he would use his key to their room late in the night, just to see that two bodies were asleep in two different beds.

"We're leaving tomorrow night. Mara, I don't want to spend our last day here together being angry. I'm sorry I called you a bitch."

"You didn't call me a bitch."

"Well, I was thinking it," Rowena giggled.

Mara rolled over in her bed. Rowena's face shone angel white in the moonbeams traveling through space to beat through the windowpane.

"I can never stay mad at you. Bitch." They both

laughed until their eyes puddled.

"I love you madly," Rowena sang.

Mara stood up and leapt over to Rowena's bed.

"I know you love Adrian, too. But do you love him more than you love me?" She kissed Rowena then, and the two melted into the mattress, removing their night clothes.

They didn't hear Dane until it was too late. He pulled Mara out of bed by her hair, and tossed her like a spare pillow onto the floor. She cried, and he kicked at her as she crawled away from him.

Rowena could only plead from beneath the sheets, naked, and shaking. "Stop it. I'm sorry. I'm so sorry, please stop."

"Shut it, Rowena." Then he walked into the bathroom and yelled, "You girls put on some fucking clothes, yeah? And hurry up about it."

"Dad, I'm sorry," Rowena sobbed, ashamed.

Dane didn't answer, but when he was certain his daughter and her lover were decent, he walked straight over to Mara and took hold of both her wrists. "If I catch you with Rowena again...carryin' on these abominable acts...I swear, girl...you'll never see Rowena again. Think on that next time you get any depraved ideas."

Mara slept alone in Dane's room that night.

After they returned home, and Mara told her parents what my dad had done, Mr. Stone beat him up. Rowena had never seen anyone stand up to her dad like that before.

•••

Tilda sat in the kitchen, drinking herbal tea while Rowena and her mother put away leftovers, and washed dishes. The men drank beer in the den, shouting obscenities at the television. When Aunt Tilly asked Rowena about Mara, Iris stiffened. "We don't speak of that wicked girl in this house. You damn well know that, Tilda."

"Bah! Mara is a darling. You and my brother have treated that lovely young woman horribly."

Iris spun around and glared at her sister-in-law, her mouth trembling. This time, she would stand up to Tilda. "If you knew what kind of woman she is, you'd see her differently."

"Please!" Tilda spat, "I do know! Do you think Dane keeps secrets from his beloved sister?"

"He promised he wouldn't tell you. I didn't want you, or anyone else to have a poor opinion of Rowena."

Aunt Tilly sipped the last of her tea, then placed both hands flat upon the table. "Turn around and face me, my girl. No. Why don't you just come here, and sit with me."

Rowena dropped the dish cloth into the hot water, and red-faced, she walked away from the sink. Iris reached out to her daughter, but was rebuked. She did as she was told, and sat in a chair across from her dear auntie. "I had no idea you knew."

"Don't look at me with those eyes. You've nothing to be ashamed of, you poor thing. Your mother is a stupid, cruel woman, and your father? Well, he's a prick," Tilda's eyes began to well—when she blinked, it was a deluge. Iris tried to excuse herself from the kitchen, but Aunt Tilly demanded that she stay. "Take a seat."

Rowena had never before witnessed Tilda cry. "What it is?"

"Have you ever wondered why I never married? Iris, haven't you ever wanted to ask? Or perhaps Dane's told you. Yes, I'm certain he has."

Iris fumbled with words, keeping her gaze squarely in her lap.

Tilda laughed, riotous for just a second. "Rowena, your mother is easily made uncomfortable, isn't she? Funny, that. Imposing distress on others is no concern of hers."

Rowena nearly pitied her mother—seeing Iris wriggle, and her pointed chin quiver so. "I've always wanted to ask why you never married. But now I think I've always known." She bit at her bottom lip a moment, considering the woman she'd admired her entire life. "Were you ever in love?"

"I was in love, once. Well, more than once, but only one was powerful enough to leave me shattered."

"You don't have to talk about this," Iris pressed. "Please, Tilda, you'll only encourage her."

But Tilda spoke louder, "Helena was her name. She had hair as black as a raven's wing. It was her hair that had struck me first. Your beauty Mara reminds me of my Helena."

The summer affair between Tilda and Helena had begun at a hot dog joint in 1966, in the city of Los Angeles. Tilda was a fresh twenty year old, traveling stateside for the first time, on her own with mum and daddy's blessing and a purse full of their money. She was instructed to return to Whitley Bay, England, once she'd worked the wantonness out of her system.

Young Tilly Summers had caused quite the scandal back home when her lesbian inclination was revealed during church service—a service she herself had interrupted, in protest of the vomitus doctrines regarding same sex relations.

Helena Carpenter was a carhop. A pert little bird, sharp of eye and tongue. She flitted about the place on white roller skates adorned with mustard yellow pompoms; Tilda stood outside the diner beneath a mid-May sun, chili dog in her hand, and utterly rapt.

"I was so taken with her, Rowena." Tilda smiled, boldly baring her aging teeth.

Iris snorted, but Rowena smiled. "Go on. What happened?"

Tilda continued with a faraway look in her eyes that melted Rowena's heart.

"I knew I had to meet her; but then what? I wanted to see her the next day, and the day after that. So I dropped my dog into the rubbish bin, and walked inside to inquire about a job. I spoke to the fry cook. He was also the owner—Raymond was his name. Well, he looked me over, asked if I could skate, and then told me to report the following Saturday for my first shift."

"You've got long legs," Helena had said, snapping her bubblegum. "That's good. You've got to be quick to keep up with me."

"I lied to Raymond. I don't know how to skate. Very well, that is."

"Shut up!"

"Truly."

Helena spat her gum. "Jesus Christ, Tilda."

"I prefer Tilly."

"So do I," Helena grinned as she continued to assess the virgin carhop. "Listen, Tilly. If you can stand up straight in skates, I can teach you to move in them without falling down and busting that deceitful English ass of yours."

"I'm sorry I wasn't altogether honest. But I need work while I'm staying here in the States."

"Don't be sorry. I'm not." And as she skated away, Helena tossed Tilda an over the shoulder wink. "Meet me back here at seven-thirty. Don't make me wait."

Helena had taught Tilda to skate at a place in Glendale on sleek maple floors, tongue and groove.

"Those late nights at the roller rink, and early shifts as a carhop were some of the greatest, and most exhausting times of my life. I'd give anything to be young again for just a moment—long enough to catch the scent of Helena's hair as she flew in circles around me." She paused to give Iris a cheeky wink. "Or a quick taste of her bubblegum."

Rowena couldn't dam her tears. "What ended the relationship?"

"My brother. Dane had been sent to retrieve me. He and your grandparents were furious when I confessed that l had moved into Helena's flat. I could have stood up against my mam and da, but not Dane. I loved him too much. I still love him too much. But you, my dear niece, you don't have to do as I do"

"Oh, Aunt Tilly." Rowena reached across the table and held Tilda's hands. "I'm so sorry. I'm angry for you." Then to her mother, she spat, "What the hell is wrong with you and Dad? You two are the real problem. Not Aunt Tilly. Not Mara. Not me."

Iris just sat and wept. *I'm never going to be a grandma.*

Tilda crossed her arms. "That's right, Iris. It's time Rowena knew the truth about me. I hope I inspire the girl to live the life that's best for her, and not for you and Dane. How dare you two attempt to dictate this poor girl's life. You should both be ashamed of yourselves. I know I am ashamed of both of you."

•••

Hey Rowena,

I ran into your darling Mara last night. I assume you're the reason she won't talk to me. I only wanted to talk to her about doing a little thing LIVE from that shithole her daddy owns. What's it called? The Crumby? Miss fucking self-righteous bitch was a total cunt to me.

What did you say to her about me??? Is this how it's gonna be now? You won't be happy until the whole damn town looks at me cross-eyed?

You can go ahead and try to make me into a pariah. Really, it's no problem. I've been around a fuck of a lot longer than you, and I have established resources. In other words—don't screw with me, baby. I know how to fuck your shit right up, and never be found out. I can go ghost-town any time I choose to.

So. Why don't you get your pretty head straightened out, and get back on board with our radio show? Yes, OUR radio show. I'll forgive everything if you'll just do that. Real truth, I'm not even pissed (maybe a little) that you put the kibosh on our FUCKING relationship. Yeah, the sex was good, but you're not irreplaceable.

Let me know what you think. You know where to find me. For the time being.

Ian

•••

Ian had been sitting at the bar in the Crumby for hours, tossing back neat bourbons when Mara came blowing in that Wednesday night, wearing the hollowness of winter on her face. Only it wasn't the cold, or the snow, or the dead white skies; it wasn't even the bizarre fright that overcame her whenever a blackbird cackled that bothered her so much.

The effects of her estrangement from Rowena were

119

brutal, at best. They'd always had a tumultuous relationship—one worth braving the waves of chaos for, even when caught up in the throes of drowning.

She often wondered, *who will break the silence this time around?*

"Mara Stone. I have a preposition for you." Ian waved an emphatic hand. "Come over here. I want to talk to you."

"Mr. Copeland," Mara greeted, approaching the bar. "I think you mean *proposition*. In either case, I'm not interested. Peddle your wares someplace else."

Ian pushed his stool away from the bar, and stood up on booze weary legs. "Listen. I want to broadcast live from Crumby."

"No. This isn't...that kind of establishment."

"Not that kind of—you're not a nice person. I mean, I've always known that. But listen, okay? This isn't for me. It's for Rowena. Okay? Rowena. Come on, Mara. You'd do anything for that bitch. I've seen you two together enough to know you'd do anything for her. That bitch."

"Ah-ha. Now I know where this proposition is coming from. Something's happened between you two." Then Mara laughed long, and riotous.

Ian took a step towards her. "What the fuck are you laughing at?" A handful of patrons turned their heads, mouths gaping; a couple of women suggested that someone locate Mr. Stone.

Mara raised her hand. No, she didn't want anyone troubling her father.

"You know what you are? You're a walking, talking, breathing piece of shit, Ian Copeland, and I will never understand what Row ever saw in you. Whatever it is she's done to you in a moment of blessed enlightenment, it is much deserved, I'm sure." She cleared her throat. "I have nothing more to say to you. Now, you can leave on your own, or I can have Robert escort you to the sidewalk."

"You fucking cunt. You can't toss me out. I didn't do anything." He jabbed a finger into her shoulder, and prompted a rather handsome man at the far end of the bar to stand up. Mara flashed the man her cocoa daggers.

"Ian, you're fucking inebriated, and I'm cutting you off. I'll call you a car. You can have a yellow one, or a white one with pretty flashing lights on top. Up to you."

And so an agreement was reached. Ian would wait outside for a yellow car to pick him up and drive him home. While Mara stood in the foyer, watching to see that Ian left in the cab she'd called, the rather handsome man walked up on her, and tapped her shoulder.

She spun on her heel. "Adrian, leave me alone, will you? Go home to your wife."

"I'm going. I only wanted to say that one of these days, your pride is going to get you in some real fucking trouble. If something ever happened to you...it would kill Rowena."

"Something's going to happen to us all, Adrian."

"Shut up. You know what I mean."

"Don't worry about me getting into trouble. Row's the one who walks straight into the shit."

"Are you two really fighting? Rowena said you haven't talked to her in a while."

"We're not fighting. Please don't pretend you give a good goddamn."

"I do care! I hate your guts, but I still care."

"Step outside with me." Mara grabbed his coat sleeve and gently pulled. "Let's have a smoke. Out back."

In the rear parking lot, Mara searched for Adrian's pick-up truck. "Are you okay to drive?"

"I'm good, actually. I wasn't here long enough to get drunk. Unfortunately."

"You only come here to get laid, anyway."

Mara procured two cigarettes from her coat pocket and offered one to Adrian. They lit up, and stood in silence for several minutes, blowing smoke and white cold breath. Snow fell delicately. Beneath the flood lights, the giant flakes sparkled like the titty-bar glitter at Adrian's favorite club. Mara laughed, a humorless din that ricocheted. The sound startled Adrian.

"What are you laughing at?

"I hate you, too. More than you hate me. But I still care. I care that you're a shit husband. I care that you're the biggest part of Row's problem."

"What problem?"

"See? That's why you're shit. You're either oblivious, or willfully blind to the effects of your behavior. Rowena. She's in misery."

"You can fuck off straight to hell, Mara." Adrian flicked the remainder of his cigarette into the snow, and shuffled off to his truck.

Mara went back inside the Crumby, half-hoping Adrian would crash and burn.

•••

Jesus Christ, Ian. You stupid fuck, first of all, I have nothing to do with Mara dismissing you. She and I aren't even speaking at the moment, and I don't know if I'll ever be able to get her back. Not that you care. Anyway, none of my relationships are your goddamned business.

Second, you might want to rethink your plans to FUCK MY SHIT RIGHT UP, being that you've threatened me in writing. Genius. I think your brain has soaked up way too much whiskey.

122

I'm not returning to the radio show. So why don't you change out of those pissy pants you're wearing? Maybe then your wife will let you put your dick in her mouth once in a while. Let me go. And don't contact me again, or I'll be forced to use my own resources. You're not the only asshole who lives in this town. I can play, too.

Rowena

•••

Mara,

I want to let you know I've received an email from Ian, and he mentioned you. I'm going to forward it to you because he's pretty sore over me quitting the radio show, and I don't want you to experience any backlash unawares. I know you're angry with me, but I care about you, so watch yourself, okay?

I don't know about you, but today has been a reflective one for me. This is the first Christmas Eve in seven years that we won't be together in one way or another. I don't suppose I could persuade you to come by tonight. Aunt Tilly left a gift for you before she flew back to England.

Thanksgiving was interesting. Aunt Tilly told me some pretty significant things about herself that I want so badly to share with you. I know she'd want you to know, too. She's always loved you. Anyway, I'll leave the package at the backdoor. If you don't want to come inside, I'll understand.
Merry Christmas, Mara. Give my best to your mom and dad.

Row

•••

Hey Row,

Thanks for looking out for me. Rest assured, I will be extremely cautious where Ian is concerned, I promise. I'm more concerned for you, though. Follow your own advice, yeah? I don't know what you've done, but he is pretty fucking angry.

Also, thanks for letting me know about the gift from Aunt Tilly. I love that lady. I will definitely come by and pick up the package, but I won't be coming inside. I have plans with my mother tonight. I'll tell her you say Merry Christmas.

I miss you. But I'm not ready to see you yet. I hope you understand. I do still love you.

Mara

•••

Don't. Please don't go through with it. That's all Beatrix had written—her last attempt to persuade Rowena.

"What's she going on about? Read me the first email again." Lucas was paler than usual; the light of his monitor was unflattering at midnight, five hours in the future.

I should never have mentioned the emails.

"I've read it twice already. Beatrix said I shouldn't be

involved with you because of your past infidelities. She doesn't want me to end up like the others. What does that mean, Lucas?" Rowena was still unfazed, but hopelessly curious about the cryptic warning.

"Honestly, I haven't the faintest...we barely speak to one another. I don't know what's inside her head—what she thinks she knows. I mean, aside from ruining some lives...I'm ashamed to admit I've played my part in a divorce or two. But I have never done anything that would warrant such a foreboding message."

Rowena snorted. "You're ashamed, yet you pursued me even knowing I'm married."

He sucked in a breath, and blew it out slowly. "Lady, had you told me you were happily married, I would have fucked off."

She didn't believe that last remark. And she didn't care.

"So you leave tomorrow, and I will see you Friday morning." Suddenly she was beaming.

"I can't believe it. My first time in America. Makes the idea of a thirteen hour flight exciting."

"I don't know much you're going to get to see. Definitely not the best parts, staying in a shitty room so close to the airport. I don't know the area well, so don't count on me to be a great tour guide."

"I don't give a fuck if we don't go anywhere at all. I'm not crossing the Atlantic to go sightseeing. I will have the best of America's attractions wrapped in my arms for three whole days."

Three short days. How bad is it going to hurt when we have to say goodbye?

Lucas sighed—a gale blew through Rowena's headset and straight to her brain.

"I know what you're thinking, baby." His hand, just a moving picture on her monitor waved tenderly before her as he stroked the image of his Lady's face. "Let's not think of the goodbye until it's time to say..."

"I love you, Lucas."

"And I, you."

"Bye for now."

Lucas blew a kiss before he disconnected. Rowena was left to imagine the fire they'd build.

Adrian's booming interrupted her thoughts. "Are you upstairs?"

"Yes!" she boomed louder.

"Come down, will ya?"

Herald was waiting for Rowena at the bottom of the stairs. Something dead was clenched between his teeth. Another goddamned Blue jay.

"Herald! Where in Hell are you finding all of these goddamned birds? Take it from him, Addy, please!"

Adrian was already wearing a pair of old gardening gloves. "You heard your mama, Grandpa. Let me have it."

Herald dropped the dead bird and walked away, satisfied.

"And Addy, trash those gloves when you're finished."

"Yeah, no shit."

Rowena followed Adrian out the backdoor and into the neighbor's field where he tossed the bird and the gloves. "I know how they're getting into the house. At least I'm pretty sure, but I'll have to get up on the roof to check the flue."

"Oh, that does make sense." She turned around to head back to the house, but Adrian stopped her.

"Why are you so dressed up, pretty lady?"

Rowena was barely dressed at all, shivering in black leather booties, and a slinky black dress. Her hair was twisted into a sleek roll, perfectly centered at the back of her head.

"I'm going out with friends. It's Lisa's birthday. You know Lisa."

"Yeah. Her husband...Scott, he's pretty cool. Will he be there?"

"I imagine so."

His fingers fluttered against her collar bone, and her cheeks flushed with a craving for him that she hadn't felt in a long while.

"You're wearing the pendant I bought you. It looks nice. You look nice. Beautiful. You're always so beautiful, Rowena." Adrian took her hand and they started back for the house. "Maybe I should join you tonight."

"I wish our wedding anniversary had been as important."

"I know. Let me finally make it up to you. Please?"

"Addy, don't..."

"Don't what?"

"Don't wear what you normally wear when you go out. Put on some church clothes. We're going to a nice place, and coming home at a reasonable hour. So no whiskey shots tonight. No champagne. Just a couple of beers."

He allowed her dig at him to slide. Sometimes Adrian regretted that he was a colossal asshole. In fact, Adrian was so well behaved at the restaurant, affectionate and charming, no other woman existed to him. Rowena was smitten. She remembered why she'd fallen in love with him in the first place.

And she kept on remembering while they rolled around in their bed that night. More than once.

But in the dark of early morning, Rowena sneaked out of bed and into the bathroom; she had not slept one peaceful second beside her husband. In a hot shower she cried. She berated herself.

Why am I doing this?

What the fuck, Row?
Use your head.
To go on like this is madness.
Love is madness.

•••

Adrian had New Year's Eve off work, so he slept in until after eleven o'clock that Thursday morning. Rowena woke him for brunch with a gentle shake and a liar's smile.

The record player was jovial, singing oldies. Adrian's favorite. He played an invisible triangle as he walked into the kitchen with bleary eyes. He was a giant toddler letting beer toots escape through his nearly transparent cotton briefs.

"Sit down, Addy. I made you the cheese quiche you love so much." She gave him a wink.

The winter sun reflected off the fresh layer of snow and shone bright as a beacon through the undressed French doors.

"I can't sit here at the table with all this light. It's hurting my eyes."

"Take my place, then. Listen now, I have to tell you something."

Do it. Now, while he's busy chewing.

"I'm going to Detroit tomorrow. I'll be gone through the weekend. We girls are going to the casino."

"You and Mara?"

"No. Mara and I are on the outs."

Adrian sighed. "Christ, Rowena. What grade are you two in again?" he laughed. You and fucking Mara, always pulling on each other's ponytails."

Rowena sipped her tea. "It isn't funny. You're not funny."

128

"Come on! That was funny!" He shook his head and added, "You and Mara are forever in ninth fucking grade."

"And what grade are you in, Addy? Kindergarten? Walking around in your threadbare underpants, farting like a nasty little boy."

He laughed harder.

Rowena rolled her eyes. "You're an ass, Adrian."

"I'm your ass, and you love me."

I do fucking not. "Eat, will you? I woke up early to make this for you."

"Yeah, okay." He was quiet for but a moment. "If we're lucky enough to get pregnant again, what would you want to name our baby?"

"I hate it when men say *we're pregnant*, or *we're trying to get pregnant*. Men don't carry babies, Adrian. It's the woman's body that grows life. And it's the woman's body who suffers when that growing life dies inside of her."

"Wow. That is about the most selfish, wicked thing you have ever said to me."

Adrian stood, kicking the chair hard enough for it to tumble into the living room.

"You think I didn't feel anything when we lost our baby girl? You think I don't still feel the loss?"

Rowena remained seated. She wasn't going to allow her husband to frighten her away.

"You're the reason I lost my baby. You just couldn't keep your hands to yourself." Her tone was as cold and even as her stare, and she held him captive for several minutes.

Adrian knew he was being challenged. "You stupid bitch, you'd just love it if I hit you again. Yeah, you'd fucking love it if I knocked you down on your ass. Then you could go running to your mom and dad, and they'd put you up in their fucking castle. You fucking princess.

And they would burn me alive!"

"Please. Those fucking idiots love you. They think more of you than they've ever thought of me." Rowena stood up then, and squared her shoulders. "Do it. I know you want to. I know you've always wanted to hit me. I make you so angry, don't I? Wouldn't if feel so damn good—"

The kitchen table was suddenly flipped onto its side. Shattered dishes and quiche lay scattered on the floor. There stood Adrian, the man-child in shit stinking underwear, heaving from his tantrum. Rowena didn't know whether she wanted to laugh, or cry.

"Clean this mess up, Adrian. I'm going out for a while. You'd better fix that table leg. Busting up my grandmother's table, for fuck's sake. What's the matter with you?"

"Get the hell out of here," Adrian shouted. "Don't worry. I'll take care of the table."

Rowena returned in the evening with shopping bags filled with bras and panties, and a new pair of boots. Adrian had gone out without cleaning up, and according to the note he'd left taped to the underside of the kitchen table, Rowena wouldn't see him until she returned home Sunday morning.

"Herald, your daddy is an asshole. Look at this mess."

Herald barely acknowledged Rowena's irritation, he was so busy chewing on dried up quiche.

PART THREE

2016

12

THE CRUMBY BAR

3 January

Adrian returned home just before noon on Sunday, and Rowena didn't give a good goddamn where he'd been. She certainly didn't care about the red and white roses he presented to her. All she wanted was to be left alone to revel in heartache. The parting kiss she'd shared with Lucas that morning still clung to her trembling lips, seven hours later.

"You been back for long? Shit. You definitely look like you had a good weekend."

"You're so sweet, Dear Addy." Rowena peeled herself off of the couch, and took the flowers into the kitchen. "You shouldn't have."

"Shouldn't have what? Come home?" he asked, following her.

"That, too," she said, preparing to cut the firm stems under the running faucet. "I can grow my own roses."

"What's the matter with you?"

"Where's my fucking kitchen table?"

Adrian backed off two steps, barely missing the cat. "It was broken. I chopped it up for the wood burner."

"You did not." She spun on her heel and faced him. "No way. Not my grandmother's table. Adrian. You couldn't have done something so cruel."

But he had done it. He'd chopped up the wood, and tossed the smithereens into the barn. Her grandmother's table lay in a heap atop the burn pile.

"Rowena. I'm sorry. I was angry. A little drunk. That's no excuse. I don't know what to say. I don't know what to do. I'm sorry. Tell me what you need me to do."

Rowena knelt, and she picked up a leg that had somehow remained intact.

"You need to let me go. I'll pack an overnight bag, and come back tomorrow for the rest of my things." As she walked away, Adrian reached for her.

"If you touch me. If you try to stop me, so help me, Addy. I will beat your goddamned face in with all I have left of my grandmother's table."

Dear Addy, he believed her. "I'll leave, Rowena. I did this, so I'll be the one to leave. Give you some time to cool off."

"I don't need to cool off. I need you to let me go. I want a divorce." She finally said it and meant it. No going back.

Rowena Summers-Fanning would have her autonomy. To hell with her highhanded parents.

I'm a grown ass woman, for fuck's sake.

•••

Adrian sidled up to the mahogany bar. He liked to drink uptown at The Crumby Bar & Kitchen, where the posh lady bartenders all fell over one another to serve up his Tullamore Dew, neat. But it wasn't the choice women that had first attracted Adrian to the place.

He'd followed Rowena once. Rowena, in a deep violet tea dress, escorted by that arrogant prick, Ian Copeland. When he attempted entrance to confront his wife, he was denied due to his dirt stained blue jeans and work boots.

So, Adrian decided to keep silent about what he knew of his wife's infidelity, and instead went shopping for church clothes. The next time he followed Rowena and Ian to Crumby, he was dressed smartly in brown leather loafers, white slim-fitting chino pants, and a navy blue polo shirt. He sat in a corner where he could safely spy through an everlasting silver-blue haze of cigarette smoke. Sipping bourbon from a rocks glass, Adrian absorbed the foreign landscape. It was no wonder to him that Rowena felt safe stepping out in public with another man. This bar was definitely not his scene. Yet, Adrian found himself admiring the lamps that mimicked the glow of gentle firelight, and the smell of leather, iron, and fire roasted fare.

Sunday afternoons were unremarkable at Crumby. People mostly came in for quiet glasses of wine, and fondue served with crusty bread and roasted artichokes.

"There's my guy."

Adrian looked up from his mobile phone.

"Amber." The name suited her. She had wide-set eyes the color of dark bourbon on ice. "You know what I want."

The bartender winked. "You've been coming in here for two years, and I've never seen you on a Sunday." She poured him a dram of Tullamore Dew from a brand new bottle, and slid it toward him. "Would I be mistaken if I thought I was the reason you came here today?"

The night before, Adrian had lifted Amber's black pencil skirt above her waist, and he fucked her brains out all over the blush hued settee in the Ladies'. It hadn't been the first time the two had locked themselves in the powder room for a ten minute tryst.

He dropped his gaze and said into his glass, "I'm actually meeting someone."

"Oh?" Her peach lips stiffened into a smirk.

"It's not what you think, babe." He emptied the glass, and she poured him another.

"It isn't?" She leaned in close, thick hair spilling over her shoulders. "I won't see your wife walk through those doors, will I?"

Adrian reached for an auburn curl, and tugged lightly. "Definitely not."

The glass panel doors opened mutely, and through them moved a dusky force of fortitude. She hated Adrian on a physical level, as he did her, in return. But goddamn, she was extraordinary to behold. She didn't walk, but danced. Every movement, she delivered with grace. Mara, a black swan.

Amber glanced at Mara, and straightened up instantly. "Are you here to see her?"

Adrian looked over his shoulder. "You know Mara?"

"Everyone here does. Her dad bought the Crumby last year. October. Helluva nice guy. He didn't change any of the staff."

"Oh, Amber." Mara directed a sneer toward Adrian. "Don't involve yourself with Mister Adrian Fanning. Trust me, his charms are as trustworthy as a wet paper grocery bag." And she kept on walking as she removed her blue wool coat.

"Thanks for that," he called out loud.

"No problem," she replied as she took a seat in the

nook, her back to the fireplace.

"What a bitch," Adrian mumbled. Then to Amber,

"Keep the whiskey coming. And gin and tonic for the boss. Top shelf. On my tab."

Adrian moved stiffly from the bar to join the ballerina. As he pulled out the other leather chair, Mara flipped her hair, dispersing the scent of jasmine. Adrian loved the scent of jasmine, and Mara knew it.

"Is Row all right?" She removed a small box from her handbag, and tapped out a long, skinny white cigarette. Adrian produced a lighter. He wasn't a smoker, but he was always prepared to light a bitch's cigarette. "Thank you, Addy."

"No problem. Thanks for meeting me."

Amber arrived with the drinks, and Adrian dismissed her with a cool wave of his hand.

"You don't have to pretend," the black swan remarked, blowing smoke. "I know you and Amber are...a thing. Spare me the eyes. I know you better than anyone. Can't you remember when we were friends?"

"I recall that we were more than friends." He downed his glass, and raised his arm, signaling Amber before she'd even made it back to the bar.

"Once. And I haven't fucked a man since."

"What are you saying? I turned you off men?"

"You're so fucking stupid." Mara laughed, gasping, and choking on smoke. Adrian nudged her cocktail. She took it and drank deeply. Amber stood stock still, table-side, intrigued by the nature of the relationship between her lover and her boss's daughter. Mara told the girl to bring the bottle of Tullamore Dew and leave it.

"Hold the gin and tonic, and tend to the other guests. You're excused," she added. Then to Adrian, "Rowena. Is she okay?"

"I don't know. When I left the house, she was in bed with Herald on one side of her, and a fucking table leg on the other. She just cried and swore at me."

"Fucking, duh. You destroyed her grandmother's table, you shit."

"I know. I'm a shit. Anyway, I didn't want to call her parents, so I called you."

"Calling me was the one thing you did right." Her cigarette had burned down to nothing. She tapped out another and reached for the lighter that Adrian had left on the table. "But I'm curious, Addy. *Why* did you call me? You didn't have to call anyone at all. What do you want from me?"

He wasted no time. "What's your opinion about Rowena's relationship with Ian Copeland?"

"Uh-uh. You can't imply an affair without giving me something to go on. What do you think you know about them?"

"Either you don't know anything at all, or you're enjoying the situation I'm in way too much." He poured a dram, and swallowed it whole. "Fine. I'll play. I followed Rowena and Ian here. Several times. They weren't exactly all over each other, but they were close. He was always touching her back, or brushing her hair away from her face. I didn't get the sense they were coming here on business. Anyway, I'm fairly sure that the last time they were here together was back in October. Rowena has since quit the radio show. That much I do know, because she told me the day she quit. She said Ian took the hit pretty hard. That was in November, I believe."

"October. That's funny." Mara dragged on her cigarette.

"Funny, ha-ha? Or—"

"Well, I can tell you honestly that I had no idea

Rowena and Ian were fucking each other. Not until my dad saw her with him. In October. He now owns this place, you know. Anyway, he'd caught them kissing in the rear parking lot. Rowena was pressed against her car, and Ian had a busy hand up her skirt." A humorless laugh followed. "I wish you could see yourself, Dear Addy. There's unwarranted rage in those beautiful blues of yours."

"Shut up."

"No. You've been fucking around on Row since way back when, babe. She's never been good enough for you. Yet, somehow, you're supposed to be good enough for her? Fuck you."

"Fuck me? You're just as goddamned mad as I am."

He poured a shot of whiskey into his glass, then passed it to Mara. She was keeping up.

"I know you love Rowena. You've been in love with her since we were kids."

"And you've only pretended to love her." She poured another whiskey, slammed it, and then slid her empty glass toward Adrian. "Look at us. Sharing drinks and bonding over a girl like good friends. Sweet, isn't it?"

Adrian winked. "Do you really not know where Rowena was this past weekend?"

"I really don't know."

"Why did you come over looking for her?"

"We haven't spoken in months. I wanted to see her."

"Rowena told me she was spending the weekend with some friends from work. I don't believe her. I've never even heard of the people she said she was going with. When I saw her this morning, she looked like she'd been crying. Hard. I wonder if it had anything to do with Ian."

"Let's think about it for a minute. Play out some scenarios. You go first."

"All right. So we know Rowena and Ian were having an affair. Your dad actually caught them in the act. Did Rowena see your dad, too?"

"He told me Row had seen him."

"A good reason to cut off the affair. Or keep the affair going, and just not come here anymore."

"You did say, though, that Rowena isn't working for Ian. She'd quit in November. That tells me Rowena has ended the affair and severed all contact with him. I highly doubt she was with Ian over the weekend."

"What if she didn't really quit the radio show?"

"Okay, Adrian. I'll be honest. I know she really did quit because she told me so. In an email. Anyway, I don't think she'd lie about that, simply because it would be too easy to find her out. You really never give Row any credit for how smart she is. I'd bet she's a hell of a lot smarter than you."

Adrian banged his gavel fist on the table. "You're giving her too *much* credit, Mara. She let a dude finger fuck her in a public parking lot."

Mara caught the glances and whispers bouncing off the walls, quiet wine, and fancy fondue momentarily forgotten.

"*Shhh!* Settle down."

"All right, all right. I'm sorry. Listen. Despite everything, I care about Rowena. Will you check in on her? And let me know how she's doing?"

"The way you ask makes you sound so innocent. But I know exactly what you want from me. Are you going to fight her about the divorce?"

"I haven't decided yet. All I know is...to think of my Rowena with another man...it burns."

Mara didn't think Adrian had the right to say such a thing, given his own promiscuity. Dear Addy was a shit. Shit husband. Shit friend. Shit human being. He hadn't yet decided if he was going to let Rowena divorce him. The arrogance of him was nauseating.

"I know it's painful. But you need to let her go, Addy. Just let her go."

And so this rare occasion of bonding had come to an end.

Adrian excused himself in a huff. Amber was desperate to walk him out, but Mara had one bitch of an intimidating stare. The young bartender only waved mutely to her lover as he stepped heavy toward the front doors to wait for the cab Mara had insisted on calling. Adrian, however, refused to keep his mouth shut.

"You're just a selfish dyke, Mara Stone."

The remark stung her face red, but Mara winked, raising the Tullamore Dew in salute before swigging straight from the nearly empty bottle.

13
SLUT

4 January

Santeria blared from the bathroom. Rowena sang along as she brushed her towel dried hair. Despite the separation from Lucas, and the residual prickle of the latest quarrel with Adrian, she was rather relaxed.

Then a voice traveled through the breezeway.

"Hello? Are you decent?"

Rowena pulled her robe tighter around her waist and secured the tattered belt into the tightest knot she could manage.

"Who's there?" She stepped out of the bathroom and into the kitchen brandishing her hairbrush. There she was, Mara, looking delicious and powdered sugar coated.

So Mara Stone comes calling.

"It's snowing," said the ballerina, shaking out her hair. "I did knock first."

"Oh!" Rowena retreated a moment to turn down the music; from the bathroom she called, "Help yourself to coffee! I'm just going to dress really quick!"

"Thanks!" Mara did help herself while she envisioned Rowena pulling on her panties, socks, and slacks, clasping her bra, and buttoning her blouse. She could hear her sweet Row singing the chorus of *What's Up?* Then, the music died. Rowena emerged, and even bare faced, she was the most beautiful woman Mara had ever known.

Adrian is a fucking fool.

"I don't have a dining table anymore for us to sit at and visit."

"I know." Mara shook her head. "I'm really sorry about that, Row. I know how much your family heirlooms mean to you. I really can't believe Addy was angry enough to—I mean, yeah, he's a dick, but..."

"I know. Seeing my grandmother's table busted up like that broke my heart. But, in light of what I've learned about her, I'm feeling conflicted." She gestured toward the living room. "You want to sit on the couch?"

Mara raised an eyebrow. "No. I won't stay long. It looks like you're going someplace important."

For a long moment, Rowena could only stare, all the while trying to avoid contact with those cocoa eyes she loved so much. Finally, she said, "Let's sit, for just a minute."

Mara followed Rowena into the living room and took a seat on the couch next to sleeping Herald. "Are you going to pretend that after all these months of silence, my showing up here isn't annoying to you?"

Rowena laughed as she lowered herself into Adrian's recliner. "I know this isn't your first attempt to see me. You were here over the weekend. Adrian called."

Mara blew on her coffee, then sipped. "Yes."

"And Adrian asked if you knew where I was. Even though I told him where I was going. Even though I told him you and I weren't speaking."

"Yes."

Rowena raised an eyebrow. "Why did you come to see me?"

"If you have to ask, then you really are fucking stupid, Row. I miss you. I came to see you because more than anything, you're my best friend. I just want my best friend. Please. Can't I have you back?"

"Last time we saw each other, you told me that whatever I could give you just wasn't good enough."

"I know. I know I said that. But I was wrong. Okay? I was wrong. Any part of you that you can give to me is enough. You're my best friend, for Christ's sake."

"Goddamn it, Mara. You're my best friend, too. But you're the one who ran off to New York. You're the one who played games with me about coming home. And you walked out on me again four months ago."

"Yeah, I get it. I hurt you. It's always about you, isn't it?"

"What's that supposed to mean?"

"Rowena, you're the most self-centered cunt I've ever met. You never consider other people, do you? Running around with Ian? What was that about?"

"What? Ian Copeland?"

"Quit it. Just quit it. I know all of your tells."

"I don't know what you mean, Mara."

"Please. Even if my father hadn't told me what he saw in the Crumby parking lot, and even if Adrian hadn't come to me with his suspicions—"

"Excuse me, but what are you talking about? Your dad saw what? And Addy? When did Addy come to you?"

"Your lousy husband called me up yesterday. Asked me to meet him at The Crumby Bar. He told me about the fight—that he broke your grandmother's table, and you were flipping the fuck out on him. I don't blame you. He said you threatened to beat the shit out of him." Mara laughed at that last bit.

"The Crumby Bar isn't exactly Adrian's scene." Rowena frowned. "So you met him. And?"

"Crumby *is* his scene, Row. He goes there all the time. Since following you and Ian. He digs the place. And the lady bartenders. Anyway, Adrian knows about your affair with Ian."

"I'm sorry, Mara. I don't care about Adrian. I only care that I've hurt you, again."

Mara sniffed, not altogether unmoved by Rowena's starry eyes. "I know my place. You don't have to apologize."

"I love you, my ballerina. I love you, and I'm no good for you. Why don't you go away? How is it possible that I haven't driven you away from me?"

"I'm much sicker than you are, Ms. Rowena Summers. I'm assuming you will take back your maiden name."

"Of course."

"Or you could just skip that step and go straight to Copeland."

Mara held eye contact while she sipped her coffee.

Rowena snorted. "Ian and I are quits. I dumped him months ago. And I've formally resigned from the radio show. I'm sure Addy told you that bit."

"He did, though he wonders if it's the truth. Adrian is highly suspicious of you, Row."

Rowena smiled, despite herself. "Let him wonder. The prick. I'm through with Adrian. And I'm through with Ian. I'm moving on. I *have* moved on."

"I'm sure." Mara's tone was even, though she burned inside. "Addy's never been anything but poisonous to you. I do understand how easy it is for you to cheat on him."

Rowena glanced about the room, fighting the prickles growing behind her eyes. "Mara, do you ever think of the good times we used to have? The three of us, we were the best of friends."

"It feels like ages ago. Because it was. But yeah, our friendship seemed invincible. I have lots of brilliant memories." She glanced down at Herald, and stroked his fur. "The dynamic changed when you decided to marry Addy. That's my fault, though. I'm the one who pulled away."

Rowena shrugged her iron shoulders. "It was not your fault." Nothing was ever Mara's fault. Not truly. All that woman had ever wanted out of life was to love and be loved with equal passion. All she'd ever wanted to was to be accepted. "Would you have dinner with me tonight?"

"Absolutely. I can get the best table at Crumby." Mara winked.

Rowena smiled at the jibe. "You know what? That sounds perfect. I'll meet you at eight."

"Nice. I'll see that the wine is chilled. Oh. I nearly forgot to tell you. The tutu Aunt Tilly gave me for Christmas is a hit with my students."

"I knew you'd love it. Maybe you can wear it for me sometime."

•••

Rowena had been expecting to find Mara already inside at eight o'clock, but the two met at the entrance, both having hurried up the ice-slickened sidewalk. Robert held the door, and a gust of wind ushered the women inside. Mara quickly turned and handed the doorman a hefty tip.

"Thank you, Ms. Stone."

"Robert, it's too cold tonight to stand outdoors. You

144

can do your job just as well here, inside the foyer. I trust you will be watchful."

"Yes, thank you." Robert was a tall man in his mid-forties, and he had a pleasant, baritone voice. Rowena thought he was quite handsome. Especially when he smiled at her. "Enjoy your evening, ladies."

Rowena tossed him a glance over her shoulder.

"We will, thanks," she breathed.

Mara snorted, but in good humor. "Row, do you have to eye-fuck every good looking man you see?"

"Absolutely." They shared a laugh, rubbing elbows and tripping over each other's feet.

The Crumby was busy for a Monday evening, nearing maximum capacity. Mara had arranged for a prime table in the dining room with a clear view of the great stone fire pit; the seductive flames flickered indigo, Mara's favorite color. A bottle of Cherry wine awaited in a lustrous, stainless steel bucket.

The maître d seated them, then poured two generous glasses. *Smooth Operator* piped through the speaker system.

"Tell Jonathon we're here," Mara said. "He knows what we want."

Rowena drank deeply from her glass, then asked, "What do we want?"

Mara winked, "Filet mignon, of course."

"No fondue?"

Mara laughed, "Not tonight. I'm not stingy like Ian. That prick is all talk."

"Ian is a cheap motherfucker, but he can't be as bad as Adrian."

"Actually, I've seen Adrian spend obscene amounts of money here."

"Oh?"

"Yes," Mara answered, unapologetic. "Your husband

likes Amber a lot. She's a bartender. I tried to get her fired, but my father—"

"I know who she is."

"You don't sound upset."

"Why would I be upset? I don't want the asshole."

Mara raised her glass. "Cheers!"

"Cheers!" Rowena sipped her wine, then added, "I saw my dad's attorney today. That's where I was going this morning. I started the papers to file for divorce."

"Row. Holy shit." Mara began to sweat. She unfolded her napkin, and brought it to her forehead, dabbing delicately at smooth, olive skin.

"I'm in trouble, and I don't know what to do. Mara, I have something to tell you. I hadn't planned to ever tell you...but I'm in such a mess. I need to talk to you about this, even though I know it will upset you."

Mara pursed her lips and considered Rowena's expression for a long moment. Then she stated plainly, "This has to do with a man."

"Yes."

"I'm not at all surprised. Is it Robert?"

"The doorman? No. Why would you—"

"You're a slut, Row. That's why."

Rowena winced. "Do you want to know, or not?"

"Goddamn it. Of course I do."

And so Rowena spilled everything all over the dinner table, including two glasses of fine wine.

•••

Mara leaned into the driver's side window of Rowena's car. "Do you really believe you love this guy?"

"I know I do."

"Why? Because he's a writer who gets you? Bullshit.

146

What has he done for you that I haven't?"

"It's not like that."

"Then tell me how it is, Row. Because the way I see it, this motherfucker has latched onto you for some...creepy reason, and he's manipulating you. He sounds crazy to me. You don't know him. You can't possibly know a person you've only spent a single weekend with. And those emails from his wife—come on, now. Use your head. Come home with me, please. I'm the one who loves you."

"I love you, too. Mara, I do. But I have to give this a go. I don't want to have any regrets."

"You'll always have regrets. You're human."

Rowena jabbed her key into the ignition. "You don't know Lucas. I do. He does understand me in a way you don't. He wants me to move to England and marry him. We're going to be together, and create together. He inspires me."

"He *doesn't* know you. Not like I do."

"He knows me enough."

"Really? Does he know that you're afraid to accept yourself for who you really are? Does he know you've been running away from yourself since the day you'd realized who truly makes you happy in this life?" She chuckled without humor. "I'll bet he does know, he's just too selfish a prick to admit it. Selfish prick would rather have you unhappy than not at all."

Rowena rolled up the window, and started the engine. *Der Kommissar* blared from the speakers. As she reversed out of the parking space, she mouthed the words, *I'll miss you, ballerina.*

Well, fuck you, my violin. Mara tossed a half-smoked cigarette into a snowbank and went back inside.

14

DEAD TO ME

5 January

Rowena,

Okay. So you called my bluff. Good on you. That's fine, and I'm okay. If you want to live the rest of your life as a goddamned nobody, who am I to intervene with your plans? Keep on living the farce of happy wife with Adrian.

Adrian. That asshole. Do you know he attacked me? I was minding my own business in a corner at Crumby, and that ballsy motherfucker walked right up to me and punched me in the nose. Yeah, it's broken. Good thing my face isn't my MONEY-MAKER, or I'd sue that bastard into HOMELESSNESS.

What is your problem? Why are you so STOOPID? Why can't I forget about you? Why am I so drunk? Did you ever love me?

Ian, your former fuckstick (remember me?)

•••

Rowena Fucking Fanning

I bet you're feeling mighty proud of yourself. It must make you smile, making me beg for a single word from you. Like, what? You have a gold-lined pussy? I'm no longer good enough for you? As I recall, I'm rather good at making you scream. But piss on it. You're dead to me.

Ian

•••

Ian,

Come at me one more time, and see what happens.

R

•••

Rowena stubbed out her cigarette in an overly full ashtray. "So help me," she said over her shoulder to Herald, "I'll kill that motherfucker."

The old cat jumped down from the divan and made his way toward the office door. He let out a long, low groan.

"You're right. Let's go to bed and take a nap."

Her sleep was deep, and she dreamed she was in a closed casket, neither dead nor alive. Paralyzed, Rowena could only gulp air—air in short supply. The sound of her heartbeat filled the black space. Claustrophobia reached into her chest, heavy and humming.

She awoke to find Herald asleep on her chest, but it wasn't the cat that woke her. Someone was knocking on the front door—no, banging with angry fists.

"Rowena! Here I am, coming at you! What are you going to do about it?"

"Herald, get up." She pushed him away and rolled out of bed. Minding the open curtains, she crawled to the bedroom closet. "I'll fucking show you, Ian."

Ian Copeland, drunk out of his mind, continued to assault the door. His voice clamored. "Get out here and show me what's up, you bitch!"

Rowena sneaked from the bedroom and made her way through the living room, then the kitchen. "I'm coming," she yelled before opening the backdoor.

"Too late," he answered, turning the door handle. The door was locked. "Goddamn it, get out here and talk to me!"

Click-clack! "Turn around. I want you to watch me shoot you."

"Shoot me with what? That fucking memento you carry around?"

Click-clack! "You got me. Do you have a smoke?"

Ian turned to find a 9mm pistol pointed at his head. "Yeah, sure." Bemused, he reached into his coat pocket and pulled out a soft pack of menthol cigarettes. He stuck one between his lips before handing over the whole pack. "Keep 'em."

"Thanks." Rowena tapped out a cigarette and lit up, never lowering her right arm. "You can leave," she added impatiently.

Was it fear or simply shock that caused Ian to move so

gently? Rowena couldn't tell, but she did enjoy the power she held. She kept the pistol aimed at his head as he walked down the porch steps and towards his car.

"I won't ever stop, Rowena."

"I thought I was dead to you."

He only shook his head before getting inside the Buick he'd painted blue for her.

15

NOTHING BUT PAIN

1 February

Rowena,

My lawyer told me not to come to the house while you're home. I'm not even allowed to call you. Unless I want to face harassment charges. I told him you wouldn't do that to me, but he's insisting I listen to him. How did we get to this point?

Anyway, I'm heading north for a while. I miss the lake and I'm sick of sleeping on Jake's couch. Your parents said I could rent the cabin from them for as long as I need it. Ha! I bet that pisses you off.

Addy

•••

Rowena sat at her desk with Herald vibrating in her lap. She stroked his plush head, and wept without sound. *I have the worst parents.* She opened the birthday card Aunt Tilly had sent the previous week, and read it again. *Thirty goddamned years old.*

The sob erupted from her diaphragm in a painful surge. Herald flexed his claws, lightly piercing her left thigh. The sting was comforting; though much less severe, the shrill sensation reminded Rowena of her cutting days. "Sweet Herald," she whispered, "I have to leave you for a little while." *Don't be stupid. What the fuck are you thinking?*

She ignored the nagging in her head as she looked for the soonest flight to England. "Here's one, leaving tomorrow."

"Meow."

•••

Addy,

I don't give a good goddamn where you go, or where you stay, as long as it is far away from me.
You have been nothing but pain to me.

You and my parents deserve each other.

R

16

BEGINNING OF AN END

2 February

Mara had found it impossible to refuse Herald. *It's not his fault Rowena's acting like a goddamned fool.* She'd even agreed to deliver Rowena to the airport, hoping that two weeks fully wrapped up in Lucas on his own turf would finally put an end to the foolishness. *Let him show her who he is.*

"I'll take care of your cat, and I'll do my best to deflect Adrian. But you have to know how stupid it is for you to fly off to England right now, Row. This is perfect ammunition for Adrian to use against you."

"I don't care. He can have my money. My mom and dad love Addy, for whatever reasons. He can move in with them and be their pampered prince. I'm finished with them all. I haven't even spoken to my parents since they found out about the separation."

"I don't like you staying alone in that house. Adrian could show up anytime he pleases. When you get back, I think we should discuss new living arrangements."

Rowena lifted her luggage from the trunk of Mara's car. "You still don't hate me?" *Oh, my God, why am I leaving her?*

"Oh. I do, believe me," Mara said firmly. "But I love you more."

"Take good care of my guy." *Don't fucking leave her. Don't fly to England.* Rowena swallowed her second thoughts, and kissed Mara on the cheek. "I'll miss you. I hope you know I will." And then she was gone.

Mara didn't wait around for take-off. She had too much planning to do.

"Don't worry, you old kitty. I'm going to straighten all of this shit out. There is no way in any level of Hell that I'm going to allow our girl to get deeper into this guy."

Mara rolled down the driver's side window a crack, then lit a cigarette. She exhaled three perfect smoke rings. *Who are you, really, Lucas Davies? Time to find to find out.*

•••

Rowena despised overnight flights. It was nearly impossible to fall asleep in a narrow seat cramped between two other restless bodies. But more than the physical discomfort, it was anxiousness that kept her awake this trip. The weekend she'd spent with Lucas in Detroit flickered in her head like a silent film.

Who is this woman wearing my face? Look at her grin.

Christ. Was her ballerina right? Was all of this a mistake? Rowena wondered, and the wonder sickened her stomach. She spent much of the flight bent over the toilet and vomiting, imagining Mara holding back her hair. Again, she asked herself what she was doing flying over the Atlantic.

What am I running towards? I can't believe I actually left Herald and my ballerina behind.

The plane touched down at Heathrow, and the nausea continued to nag as she maneuvered through the airport crowds. *If I can't straighten myself up, they won't let me board the fucking plane. I need to board the plane. I have to get to Newcastle.* She unbuttoned her wool coat. *Don't faint. Don't faint. Just one more flight. Get to Newcastle, and I can figure out what the fuck to do after I land. Figure out what to do? I know what to do. I came for Lucas. I love him.* She unbuttoned her cardigan. *But I love Mara, too. I fucking hate myself. Whatever I decide, it's the beginning of an end.*

17

FORGIVE ME

11 February

Rowena walked out of Newcastle International with wide eyes. "Where are you?" she spoke into her cellphone. "Oh, I see." A silver Honda Civic hailed her with one sharp honk. Rowena ran, her luggage bouncing at her heels. She saw the trunk pop open, and then the driver exited the car.

"Who are you?" Rowena clutched the collar of her coat.

"I'm John, your auntie's neighbor. Tilda's in the backseat."

"Oh?"

John smiled with his eyes. "She asked me to drive her. Here, let me take care of those." He reached for her belongings. "Go on, get in where it's warm."

"How kind of you, John." She opened the door, wary, and peered inside the sedan.

"You're letting the heat out," Aunt Tilly scolded. "Get in here, you daft girl."

"Oh, thank God," Rowena breathed. She slid in beside Tilda and buckled her seatbelt.

Leaving the car park, Rowena thought she heard her name roaring beneath the planes. She turned around to look through the rear window, and there stood Lucas, stone cold and brimming with blackness.

My God. What have I done? Forgive me.

•••

Lucas,

I know I owe you an explanation. I'm just not ready to talk to you yet. Those voicemail messages you left have made me nervous. You're angry, and I understand. But the things you said are terrible. The threats you're making against me are ridiculous. I had no idea you could be so hateful. To me, at least.

Can you just give me a few days, please? I need to get my shit together. I promise I will explain. I'm so sorry. It's just that I've finally accepted who I am. And I'm not for you.

Rowena

•••

Lady, I'm not waiting around for you to decide when I'm worthy of your time.

Fuck you.

I phoned your landline to speak to your husband.

Unfortunately, no one picked up. I left a message for Adrian on the answer machine. Don't know if he'll give a damn or not.

All I know is I won't let you get away unscathed for humiliating me. I thought you knew better than to fuck me over, babe.

Lucas

•••

Rowena closed her netbook. She stared at the guest bed decked with family quilts and feather pillows. Shattered from all her crying, she only wanted to settle down deep beneath the covers, and phone Mara. She only wanted to admit out loud that her ballerina had been right all along.

All-a-fucking-long.

"Rowena! Are you going to join me for tea, or not?" Aunt Tilly's voice traveled up the stairs and penetrated the bedroom door.

Rowena slinked down to the kitchen, utterly deflated. "I'm sorry. I was just going to call up Mara. I want to let her know what's happening."

"Don't worry about Mara. I've already spoken to her. She knows you're safe, and that's what's important. She's expecting to hear from you a bit later. You can phone her after we've had our tea. After you've told me what in hell you've gotten up to."

"You spoke to her? When? What did she say?"

"Are you trying to catch flies? Close your mouth. Of course I rang Mara straight away. You had me worried."

"Oh, Aunt Tilly." Rowena ran into her auntie's arms, and sobbed, "I'm a fucking mess. I've hurt people, and I don't know what to do. I'm so fucking scared."

Tilda's old hands stroked the length of her niece's hair. "I know the feeling all too well. Sit down. Tell me everything."

"Mind if I smoke?"

"If it will get you talking, I don't mind. Come on with it, now."

Rowena lit a menthol cigarette. She exhaled a thin stream of smoke. "It was as if no time had passed since we last saw each other. Our connection is something out of this world. His parents even noticed…oh, Aunt Tilly! His parents are lovely people. They made me feel like I was home. And I was. I was home in Lucas' arms, but still, I couldn't help thinking about my ballerina. I was sneaking phone calls in the middle of the night so I could hear Mara's voice if only for a few minutes. I'm cursed! To be in love with two people is fucking torture." She paused a moment to drag on her cigarette. Tilda sipped her tea, waiting. "Lucas proposed. I said yes." Choked laughter erupted between them.

"You daft girl."

"I said yes." Rowena's laughter deepened, rising from her gut. Tears ran heavy, dripping from her chin, and her shoulders heaved. "I said yes, and then I ran out on him." She reached into her front jeans pocket and pulled out a sapphire ring. She tossed it onto the table, and Tilda picked it up.

"You kept the ring?"

"I wasn't thinking clearly. All I was focused on was getting away from Lucas and back to Mara."

Tilda grasped her niece's hand. "Rowena, has Lucas hurt you? Is he violent?"

"No! Nothing like that. It was something Mara told me last night. I couldn't get it out of my head. She told me she'd been in contact with Beatrix. That's Lucas' wife. Well, soon to be ex-wife. Anyway, Beatrix told Mara about Lucas' prior extramarital relationships. There have been several, and all of those relationships had been with American women. The woman before me committed suicide only weeks before Lucas flew over to meet me. There was a note. All it said was *goodbye, Lucas.* I guess that's why Beatrix made such efforts to deter me from continuing with Lucas."

"What efforts, dear?"

"A few emails. She told me Lucas had *taken a shine* to other American women. She must feel guilty for never reaching out to the others, especially the dead one. Oh, my God."

"That's a little crass, the dead one. But you're right, I think, about Beatrix feeling guilt."

Rowena picked up her lighter. *Click-clack! Click-clack!* "I wonder why Beatrix stayed with Lucas for all these years," she wondered aloud. *Click-clack!*

"Sometimes we must resign ourselves to the fact that we won't always get the answers we seek. Let's just be glad you are no longer involved with that awful man. There's someone back home that's perfect for you, and she's waiting. Why Mara has put up with you all these years, I don't know."

"I don't deserve her, Aunt Tilly."

"Not with that attitude!"

Rowena let out a long sigh. "My attitude. You're right. I need to get home right away. Thank you for coming to my rescue, Aunt Tilly. Thank you for loving me."

"I'd do anything for you. Even though you deserve a spanking at times. Let this be a lesson to you. Promise me you'll take better care of the ones you love. Take care of Mara."

"I have a lot to atone for, and I'm scared as hell. But I'll do it, I promise."

"Good girl. Now go phone Mara and book your flight."

18

ONE CRUEL LADY

13 February

Rowena hugged her auntie, and kissed both of her cheeks. "Will we see you for Thanksgiving?"

"Perhaps not. It's no holiday of mine, and there's never any mushy peas." Tilda allowed a chuckle to escape her mouth, and then added, "I'm growing too tired to make the journey, if I'm being honest."

"Fair enough. How about Mara and I come to you for Christmas?"

"Please do. That would make my heart smile."

"I love you, Aunt Tilly."

"I love you, too, my darling girl. Off with you, now."

Rowena didn't look back at the silver Civic, and John didn't waste a minute.

The airport lounge was crowded, and it smelled like cheese on the brink of turning. Rowena found a seat between two disgruntled men in posh suits. One of them was shouting into his cellphone, and the other was using his fingertips to beat the shit out of his laptop.

Rowena pulled out her netbook, and accessed her email account. The inbox was ablaze with wrathful mail from Lucas.

•••

Rowena,

What interesting conversations I've been having with your husband. So you've snagged Ian, as well, eh? I'm impressed. It appears you're a very active temptress. Has Adrian contacted you yet? You know he actually wants to work things out with you? He's just as pathetic as I am. What really kills me is that my biggest threat has always been your precious ballerina. If you'd only told me the truth about you two, I could have accepted her— welcomed her into our relationship. I would have done anything you wanted if it meant I could keep you.

Does she even know about me? Is it her fault you decided (rather suddenly) I wasn't worthy of you? Or perhaps Mara's just another stiff caught in your web. You are one cruel lady. What are you going to do when Reckoning comes calling on you? You must know that the day will find you when you are finally at your happiest. And I feel sorry for you. I feel sorrier for you, than I do for myself.

Lucas

•••

Lucas,

I told you I would give you an explanation. I just needed a little time to sort myself out. Now, I don't think you deserve one. I hope it makes you feel good, frightening me. I never thought you would be the kind of man who threatens a woman. Oh, what I have learned about you!

•••

That you think I care about any explanation from you makes me laugh. You're so full of yourself. I hate you. And I can't wait for the day you get yours. I only wish I could be there to see it happen. Who knows? Maybe I will.

L

19

IMPORTED RED ROSES

14 February

She demanded to go home. "I have to know what damage has been done."

"You don't want to see it. Trust me, it's ugly." Mara lit two cigarettes at once, and passed one to Rowena. "I know you don't like my fancy-lady skinny ciggies."

"It's fine. I'll take what I can get right now. Thanks." She dragged hard, then rolled down the passenger window a bit. Cold air hummed in her ear.

"I told you I'd pull off to a gas station—"

"No." Rowena inhaled...exhaled. "I just want to get far away from the airport as quickly as possible. Don't stop until we get home."

Mara persisted. "Why not go straight to my place? Herald misses you. I'll take you home in the morning so you can pack what's left of your things. You're staying with me at my apartment until we find another place."

"I'm going tonight. With or without you."

Rather than argue, Mara turned up the radio. Bruce Springsteen sang *Hungry Heart.*

The Fanning house stood proudly atop a slight hill, and the moonlight offered no indication of damage. Rowena thought Mara had embellished the details. She unbuckled her seat belt, feeling relieved.

"I was expecting a pile of rubble."

"Just wait."

Mara drove around to the back of the house. The picture window was absent of glass. A kind police officer had taped up plastic to protect against the elements and stray animals. Shards of windowpane were scattered upon the patio, and among the mess lay the motion sensor light, busted.

Rowena unlocked the backdoor, and stepped lightly into the breezeway. The redolence of stale beer and human piss quickly began to circulate. She flipped the light switch on and off, on and off.

"No goddamned lights." She flipped the switch several times more. "No lights."

"Here." Mara reached into her handbag, and handed Rowena a mini flashlight. "The lights are all smashed throughout the house."

"And you really don't believe that Adrian did this?"

"No, I told you. The police called him up—you know they have that prick on speed dial by now. Anyway, he asked them to get a hold of me. He told them he was in Maine. They even traced the call, Row. Listen to me, Adrian isn't responsible. He'd even lied and said you were with him, and that I was keeping an eye on your house, for fuck's sake."

"Maine? He told me he was going north to my parents' cabin. I'm so confused, Mara. When you did speak to Adrian, did he say when he was coming home?"

"Yeah. He said he'd be back by Sunday. He sounded angry that he had to return so soon."

Rowena made her way toward the kitchen door. "It fucking stinks in here," she remarked over her shoulder.

Mara lit a cigarette, and exhaled loudly. "Be ready, Row. It only gets worse."

The kitchen cupboards Adrian had built were all splintered. They'd been axed with much passion. Dishes were strewn in pieces, more heirlooms, destroyed. The refrigerator lay on its side, doors wide open. Mara had already cleaned up the spilled contents, but remnants of vanilla bean ice cream remained stuck to the floor. Rowena groaned, and went for a rag.

"Look at this."

"Leave it, Row. We'll worry about cleaning up tomorrow. Let's get out of here."

Rowena shrugged off Mara's gentle hands, and entered the living room. "Oh! Adrian's not responsible? Why is the answering machine broken to bits?"

"Why would the broken machine connect to Adrian?"

"Because Lucas told me he'd called and left a message on my machine specifically for Adrian. And he told me they've been in contact with each other. Who else would be angry enough to—"

"He's in Maine. He probably called the machine direct to check for new messages."

"Maybe. I mean, that's a good possibility. Though I still don't believe he's in Maine."

"Why not? Most of his family is there. I'll bet he lied to you to make it more difficult for you to serve him with divorce papers."

"Now *that* make sense."

"See? Do you want to know who I think it was?"

Rowena pointed the flashlight at Mara.

"Ian." Her voice was cold, and heavy as stone. "Ian did this."

"Ian Motherfucking Copeland," Mara stated with confidence.

"I'm going to throw up."

"No, you're not. Go outside and get some air while I pack you a bag."

"I have enough clothes already in my luggage. Right now, I just want my computer."

"I never did go upstairs. I hope it's still standing. I'll be right back."

"Wait. I'm coming up with you."

They found the tower mostly intact. Taped to the shattered monitor was a note:

You're dead to me.

But perhaps most unsettling were the dozens of imported red roses that decorated Rowena's office.

•••

Rowena lay asleep on the futon with Herald, and Mara stared out the window, her eyes fixed static on the river. While the water flowed freely, the banks still wore the white mantle of winter. Spring was a long way off. She sipped her coffee, but it did nothing to warm away the chill in her bones.

How much deeper into hell will I walk for you, Row? All the way.

Mara blew hot breath onto the windowpane, and with a light touch, she drew a heart.

20

TOTALLY UNGLUED

15 February

Rowena rested her head in Mara's lap. "I can't press charges against Ian if I'm not willing to provide any evidence that he's harassing me. I refuse to turn my computer over to the police. I'm ashamed enough as it is for the way I've carried on. Jesus. What would my parents say?"

Mara scoffed, "Piss on your parents."

Rowena sat up, and leaned into Mara until they were nose to nose. "I'm sorry, my ballerina. I'm sorry for the way I've treated you through the years. I'm so in love with you. It's always been you."

"You're not going to make me cry," Mara snorted. And she kissed her violin with tear wetted lips.

•••

Rowena and Mara met Adrian at the Fanning residence at

noon. The destruction screamed in the daylight. Holes in walls and doors, molested artwork, and burned family photographs were now a stain on Rowena's heart.

Adrian kicked a kitchen chair across the room. "You know who did this it, right?"

Rowena answered, "Ian Copeland. Mara thinks we should press charges."

"No. I don't want the goddamned hassle. Not now, on top of going through a fucking divorce," he huffed. "We'll go to the station tomorrow—you and I—and file a report. Don't worry. I'll take care of Ian myself."

"You will? When? What are you going to do?" Mara wondered out loud. "Row is vulnerable. I don't understand why you both refuse to burn his ass. What if Ian's only getting started?"

"Well, it looks like you and *Row* need to leave town." Then he looked straight at Rowena. "You really fucked up this time."

"Addy—"

"Shut up and listen to me. You've got two—no, three guys totally unglued, and one of them's threatened you. Get the fuck out of town. Walk away from this house, don't fight me for anything, and I'll leave you alone."

Rowena nodded. "Fair enough. I just have one favor to ask. I need you to get rid of something for me."

21
FOOLISH

1 March

Rowena,

I know it's been ages. Don't think I'm writing to rekindle whatever it was we had between us. (What was it we had between us?) I only want you to know that I saw Lucas at a pub recently, and he was ranting about an American woman who shattered his life.

We're not mates anymore, he and I, so I didn't speak to him. In fact I left the pub before he even noticed me. I'm only telling you this because I thought I was in love with you for a while, and I don't want to see you hurt. I've seen too many women hurt by Lucas. I don't want to scare you.

No. I do want to scare you, actually.

I know that whatever you did to Lucas must have been

pretty rotten. I'm certain he deserved it, though. I'm not asking you to tell me anything. In fact, I'd prefer if you didn't. I've moved on with my life, and I'm quite happy. I hope you will be, too, someday. Take care of yourself.

Connor

•••

"I've been thinking. Instead of moving out of town, we should move out of Michigan altogether. Felicia has real estate connections all over the place." Mara frowned. "When Adrian said we should leave East Hampton, I think he meant further than ten miles out of town."

"Your mother found the perfect house for us already. And you don't want to leave Boyd's again." Rowena finished taping up the box she'd been packing, then lit a cigarette.

"No. But I hate the country. All the bugs, and snakes. Please don't make me move to an old farmhouse. It's spooky and too secluded."

Amused, Rowena snorted, and coughed out smoke. "I don't believe I've ever heard you whine before."

"I never whine. I only implore."

"I shouldn't have shown you Connor's email. You're all worked up. Listen, there's nothing Lucas can do to me from England."

"I don't know if you're really this brave, or faking it. Either way, I wish you'd stop being so stupid."

Rowena blushed, and spat, "I'm not fucking stupid!"

"Really? Then why did you hand your computer over to *Adrian* of all people? He's been nothing but cruel to you, Row, and after everything he's done, I can't believe you actually trusted him to destroy it."

"You're still banging on about my computer? Christ, Mara. Addy knows how to make all of that shit disappear."

"So do I. With a baseball bat and a bonfire," she choked. "Row. I don't trust Adrian. I'm actually afraid. Afraid of everyone involved. Ian. Lucas. And especially Addy."

Rowena pursed her lips and blew a final gust of silver smoke from her nostrils as she extinguished her cigarette. "I'm not afraid. I'm just angry."

"I hope that anger doesn't get us into more fucking trouble."

"Come here," Rowena winked. "I've got some trouble for you."

Mara went to her. She never could refuse her violin.

22

THE PROPOSAL

31 March

It was a grand farmhouse painted pale yellow, nearly one hundred years old, and boasted enough modern updates to appease Mara. Herald adapted easily. There were many sunny windows to enjoy, but his favorite place to lounge about was in the great bay that extended from the peninsula kitchen. From the window seat, he had a prime view of the sprawling plot that the woman he loved so well would fill up with roses.

"Let's plan a garden wedding."

"Row?"

"Listen." Tall and sinewy, stood up from the porch swing.

Mara covered her mouth with her gloved hands as Rowena bent a knee in one fluid movement.

She could have been a dancer, too, Mara thought.

Rowena exhaled between smiling teeth; the air was just cold enough that her breath puffed out in plumes of ghostly white. Early morning sun reflected off her hair, blushing yellow light. And those eyes of hers, they glittered like blue ice, ablaze.

"What are you doing?" Mara whispered.

"I don't have a ring. All I have is my heart. I love you, and I want you to have it, always. Will you accept my heart, Mara?"

"Your heart is all I've ever wanted. Yes, let's fill the garden with roses and get married."

"I'm sorry it's taken me this long."

"I would have waited forever. But I'm glad I don't have to."

"Glad. Just glad?" Rowena smirked in good humor.

Mara reached for the back of Rowena's head, and pulled her in for kiss. The flavor of menthol cigarettes and black coffee melted into her tongue. She murmured against Rowena's lips, "Let's go inside. I want to have a real taste of you."

23

A BLUE OLDSMOBILE

1 April

April came in with a rain of disgust. Much of Rowena's family had sent back decline cards. Her parents' refusal to attend the ceremony had been the most venomous.

"You are not a lesbian," Iris demanded. "Your father and I have arranged a prayer group. Our church family wants to welcome you back, Rowena. Please, come to the meetings, and let us help you."

"I love Mara. I'm going to marry her."

"God will not recognize your marriage."

Rowena quit pacing, and sat down at the kitchen table. "We will marry in our garden under the blessed eye of the sun."

"Your wedding won't be a celebration. The day you marry Mara will be your funeral in our eyes. You dad and I cannot abide this marriage."

"I don't need you and Dad. I have Aunt Tilly."

"Tilda! This is all her fault, anyway."

"Goodbye, Mom." Rowena hung up and wept. "I need to call my aunt."

"We are planning a late June wedding. I know you said that your traveling days were over, but it will mean the world to me if you'd give me away."

"Of course, I'll give you away," Tilda told her niece over the phone. "You daft girl. It'd be an honor. You've made me a proud auntie. I love you, Rowena. And don't give another thought to what your dreadful mother said to you."

But Rowena could help but dwell on the conversation she had with her mother.

•••

Mara brushed the hair away from Rowena's neck, and kissed the soft flesh behind her ear. "Fuck them," she murmured.

Rowena pulled Mara into her lap. "And fuck this town. You were right. We should have cut it out of here. The people are awful—I can't get a caterer to talk to me."

"I don't want to be right." Mara's eyes went glassy. "I don't—"

"Let's elope. We'll take our wedding to Aunt Tilly."

Mara jumped up and beamed. "Yes, and let's surprise her. We'll fly out when I get back from New York. Oh, I wish I didn't even have to go."

"Well, you can't keep paying for that goddamned apartment. Go out there, sign the papers, and turn right around for home."

Mara lit a cigarette, and then she plugged in some information on her mobile phone. "We can get a flight to Heathrow on Monday after I return. That would be the thirteenth."

178

"Perfect! Aunt Tilly will be so happy."

"You know," Mara offered, "I could go to New York early. Break my lease."

"No. The cost of breaking your lease is more than the rent for the next two months would cost. Go in June when the lease is up, and then we'll go get married!"

"I fucking adore you. Let's do it."

"Oh, but what about Herald?"

The old cat yawned at the sound of his name, and he hopped down from the darkening window seat. The moon would soon be rising. He rubbed his big head against Rowena's calves. She felt Herald's vibrations through the material of her pants.

"I'm sure my mom will come stay with Herald." Mara reached down and scratched the fella's head. "He loves Felicia. Don't you, you little—wait? What's that sound?" She stood up and went to the bay window. "Holy fuck, Row. Look at this."

A blue Olds tore around the side of the house, straight through the backyard. The tires peeled up the earth and kicked it all over the front of garden shed. The driver had taken out several prize roses bushes, and Rowena couldn't stop screaming.

"Who the fuck?" she shouted at Mara.

"I'm getting the gun." Mara ran to their bedroom and retrieved her dad's old revolver.

The driver was still outside ripping up the garden. She ran out the backdoor and fired a warning shot. The Olds slid to a stop, engine revving. Mara took aim for a rear tire, but missed. The bullet shot through the trunk. She fired again with the same result.

"Shit!"

Rowena opened the window and shouted, "I have 911 on the line! Get inside!"

As Mara raised the gun a third time, the Olds sped away, leaving two muddy trails.

"He killed my flowers. Some of those I've had for years."

Mara raised an eyebrow. "Goddamn Ian. I'm going to see that motherfucker pay."

24

BAIL

Mara poured herself a cup of morning coffee. "Can you believe Ian made bail?"

"Yeah, actually. I'm more surprised they didn't haul your ass in for shooting at him."

"Row, you have to come to New York with me."

"I hate New York more than you do." Rowena sighed. "I know you're right, but I refuse to run away scared."

"*Be* scared, for fuck's sake." Mara allowed herself to weep. "I can't go knowing you're in danger."

"How about I go stay with your mom? Would that ease your worry?"

"It's better than nothing. But if you're going to stay with Felicia, you *stay* with her. Don't be coming home during the day to fuck around in the garden."

Rowena grinned. "You know me too damn well."

Mara put her arms around Rowena and stood up on her tip-toes. Their lips crashed together, and they kissed each other like it was the first time.

"I love you," Rowena whispered, her voice on the edge of trembling.

Mara pulled her t-shirt over her head, and then unbuttoned her jeans, exposing her dark flesh. "I love you, too."

Rowena combed her fingers through her hair, releasing the scent of her sandalwood rose shampoo. Mara bit her bottom lip as she watched her violin strip to the sound of the concerto playing on the record player.

"Dance for me?" Rowena asked.

And Mara danced.

25

MY LADY

14 May

Dear Rowena,

I miss you, and I'm sorry for all the horrid things I said to you. I was hurt (rightly so). But I cannot live the rest of my life in this awful mental state. I can never unknow you, remember?

Can you forgive me?

Lucas

•••

Dear Lucas,

I never thought I'd hear from you again. I'm sorry for running out on you. I wanted to explain myself, but you

wouldn't let me.
I can forgive you, but I can't see you again. I'm going to marry Mara. I've always been hers, and she, mine.

Rowena

•••

Rowena, my Lady

I'm coming for you, my Lady. I just need a few months to get my affairs in order.

•••

You don't know where to find me.

•••

Trust me, Rowena, I do know. There isn't anything or anyone on this earth capable of keeping me away from you.

Always yours,

Lucas

26

ALWAYS YOURS

10 June

Rowena awoke alone. Lucas was gone. All that he had left behind was a note taped to the headboard of the bed:

Thanks for the lighter. I'll be seeing you. Always yours, Lucas.

She sobbed into her pillow. Images of their indiscretion flooded her, and she beat her fist against the mattress. How could she have betrayed Mara?

•••

He'd shown up in a taxi early that morning. Rowena was sitting on the front deck, enjoying a hot cup of coffee. Oh, the sight of him!

"Lady, I've missed you," he said quietly as he ascended the steps.

"I can't believe you found me."

"I told you there isn't anything or anyone on this earth capable of keeping me away from you."

Rowena approached him, and fell into his arms. He held her tightly for a moment, inhaling the scent of her hair.

"Lucas, I'm going to marry Mara."

He pulled away from the embrace, and placed his hands upon her shoulders. "I'm not here to change to your mind."

"Why then? Why come all this way?"

Lucas kissed her, and her body responded with heavy desire. She leaned into him, gently grinding her hips against his.

"Take me to your bedroom, Lady."

She opened the front door. "Why can't I resist you?"

He pushed her inside the house, and kicked the door closed behind them. "We're fated to be together." His hands wrapped around her throat. He squeezed until she released a tiny squawk and tapped him on the arm. Slowly, he loosened his grip.

Rowena seemed mostly unbothered as she directed him to her bedroom. "Not so rough," she said as she pushed Lucas down onto the bed.

"I'll be good, I promise. Now strip."

She began to pull her night shirt over her head, but abruptly stopped. "Do you want to have some real fun? Let me have your phone."

"It's in my front pocket. Take it. Take anything you want from me."

•••

"I'll never tell her," Rowena swore aloud.

But the videos! What was I thinking? What if he...oh my God, Mara. I'm so sorry I'm so fucked up. You won't forgive me this time. You can never find out. Never see who I really am.

27

SCRATCH OF A WHISPER

Rowena:

11 June

For as long as I can remember, I've wondered how it would feel to have a knife thrust into my gut. When I was a kid, I washed dishes after dinner to earn an allowance, only I wasn't allowed to touch the sharp knives. Mom or Dad would wash those later. But when no one was looking, I *would* touch the knives. I'd take the handle of a steak knife, or a paring knife, and point the blade inward, lightly pressing the tip into my belly button.

Now that I've had a dagger thrust into my belly, I can absolutely say it's a fucking awful sensation. It's the kind of pain so impressively brutal, it hasn't yet allowed me to cry out. I want to—I need to howl—but maybe I won't have the chance.

Jesus! I can hear Herald crying. He must be so scared. *I'm* so scared.

My skin prickled upon the piercing. And all of my innards began to itch and burn the deeper the blade was plunged.

How did this happen?

Play it back, play it back...

I didn't scream or start when I caught her walking up. I was kneeling in my flower garden. I only gasped, as she was on me before I could stand, but she didn't stick me right away.

First, she said—no, she mocked, "I can never unknow you." Her skin smelled of posh French perfume, and her breath was heavy with Irish whiskey—the good stuff. I can't smell anything now except the dirt and my blood.

She forced me onto my feet by the nape of my neck. She stuck me then, and I dropped my trowel.

Goddamn it. Why didn't I use my trowel on her?

When I felt the hilt of the blade press against me, I looked up into her dark eyes. I thought she would totally gut me. I wanted her to do it. But she didn't. That's how much she must hate me. I've been bleeding to death in my own motherfucking backyard ever since.

I'm cold, and quite lightheaded.

Nauseated.

Above me the silver maples are waving their branches. So lovely. The underside of uncountable leaves twinkle like stars shining against the backdrop of blue. The clouds are bleached white, and the summer sun is looking directly upon us. She's lying beside me, running her red tacky fingers through my hair. If not for my life leaking out of me, staining my clothes and the grass all around me, I would think it a rather romantic scene.

I don't want to see any more of the world I'm about to leave behind. I must close my eyes.

I'm going to die.

I'm going to fucking die here with no one at my side but this madwoman.

I can't go out mutely. I won't. "Goddamn you." Only a scratch of a whisper, but I know she heard me.

She has her hands wrapped up in my matted and sticky hair, and she's sobbing all over my face. Or maybe those are my own tears rolling hotly down my cheeks, my neck.

Dear God, how did my life end up like this?

Forgive me.

28
1970 442

16 June

Ian's wife returned home a day early after a brief stay at her sister's, and found her husband in the garage, dead in the driver's seat of his 1970 442, newly rebuilt. His skin had turned a comparable shade of blue.

Though she'd often imagined the sight of his splattered brains, Mrs. Copeland wasn't prepared to know the grotesque truth of her fantasy. As if Ian hadn't humiliated his wife enough, the sight of his head blown out caused her to vomit all over the garage floor.

"Perhaps your husband killed Rowena Fanning, and couldn't handle the guilt? It's not outside the realm of possibility."

"I know Ian loved Rowena," she told the police officer. "She broke his heart. Maybe he did kill her. But he *didn't* kill himself. Ian hated guns. And anyway, the bastard wasn't left-handed."

29

THE KILLING HOLIDAY

Mara:

17 June

I'm coming for you, Cinnamon Devil. I'll see to it that you pay for all the hurt you caused Rowena. And I'll take my time about it. The killing holiday.

I know exactly where to look for you. I found the postcard hidden at the bottom of her memory box. The one with the shitty poem you'd scribbled at the bottom.

> *My heart, it does bleed;*
> *your love has killed me—*
> *a murder amongst roses*

Fuck you. It's my heart bleeding to death.
She'd always been mine. Never yours.
For you, Rowena. I'll do it for you.

192

30

THE LOST KNIFE

10 October

1:00 a.m.

"Mara, what are you playing at?"
"I've been dying to show you something. Sit tight."
"Tell me what you're playing at, damn it!"
She smiled, fondling the lighter.
Click. Clack.
Click. Clack.

•••

Lucas sat on the bed, hunched over Mara's laptop, poring over familiar contents, courtesy of a generic flash drive. Mara paced the room, smoking, watching. Every so often he'd huff, or tug on his earlobes; they grew redder by the minute.

"I had a feeling this would upset you." Mara sat down beside Lucas, and offered him a drag of her cigarette.

"Thanks." He smoked, never taking his eyes off of her. "Do you want this back?"

"You can finish it. I've had enough." She stood up and stretched. "I'm going to get dressed. And you should at least put on your pants."

He dragged hard on the last hit, then tossed the dead cigarette into the plastic cup. "Why's that, babe?"

Mara pulled a tee-shirt over her head, and answered, "Because killing a man while his cock is out would be distasteful."

They both laughed.

"You don't want to kill me. You've fallen for me," he chided. Still, he moved from the bed and collected his clothes. "Mind if I shower?"

"I do mind. Come on, now. Put your dick away." She pulled on a pair of jeans, then sat in the desk chair to shoe her feet.

"You're taking the piss."

Mara was not taking the piss. She reached for her handbag. Lucas began to dress in haste.

"You love me," he insisted.

"You recorded yourself fucking my fiancé the day before she died."

"Beatrix just willingly handed over—"

"She was more than accommodating. Bet you didn't know that your sweet, agreeable wife was so computer savvy. Or that she was capable of killing. "

He made a move towards her. "Forget Beatrix. Forget Adrian. You love me. Don't lie, Lady. We can put this behind us."

Mara pressed, "You had been plotting with Adrian. What happened? You were supposed to kill Rowena on

June tenth. Instead, you fucked her and ran out. Why?”

"I couldn't go through with it.”

“That's what Adrian figured. He knew Beatrix could. He knew that she would. He paid her a lot of money to do something he himself couldn't fucking stomach to do. Not that Beatrix really wanted the money. She would have done it for free. In fact, I read the emails between Beatrix and Adrian. She admitted that she'd been entertaining the idea of murdering Rowena.” She sighed. “You'll be much more difficult to kill than Ian.”

Lucas sank down onto the bed, pale and sweating. “Hold on a minute. You told me that Ian committed suicide.”

“No, I didn't.”

“Yes! At Tokyo. You told me—”

“I admit I'd left it open-ended just so I could gauge your response. Your last email exchange with Adrian was June ninth. I believed your reaction when I told you about Ian. You didn't know he was dead.”

“Then believe me now, I swear to the gods, I love you. I still love you.”

“And I swear to your gods that you were next, Lucas. I did a lot of investigating. Adrian was going to have you killed. Then me. Of course he'd save me for last.”

“I loved Rowena, goddamn it. And now, I love *you*. Mara. I know you love *me*. Let's run away and hide. I'll keep you safe. Adrian will never be able to find us.”

“I can't love you. I *don't* love you.” she said, jamming a fist into her handbag.

“You love me.”

“You're dead. And so is your wife.”

He stood up from the bed and approached her.

•••

195

The room had developed a robust bodily odor. She didn't mind, though, and neither did her lover.

Sound and Color streamed through her earbuds. She lay down on the floor, musing a moment at the smoke rings that rose from her expertly formed lips and disappeared into the ceiling. "Impressive form, wouldn't you say?"

The indifference of his fixed stare was belied by the unending wonder of his gaping mouth. For good or for ill, he'd never been a man capable of holding back his emotions.

She'd been taken by surprise, as well, for the blood spray had been much grander than anticipated; without aiming, she managed to bury the blade deep inside the it-spot of his neck. He landed like a felled tree, and the floor trembled.

Well pleased with herself, she took a final drag of her menthol cigarette, and blew smoke at his perfect face, splashed with crimson death. *Sound and Color* faded out and into *Glycerine*. Her breath hitched at a memory, and she reached for him.

"See?" she whispered, dragging her long left index finger down his cheek. "I fucking told you so."

31

PRETTY WHITE BLOUSE

10 October

9:00 a.m.

The dining room was dimly sunlit, as the curtains were only half open. Mara seated herself at the head of the table and took a sip of lukewarm tea. Beside the tea cup, a cigarette burned away in a glass ashtray.

"Mind if I bum a smoke?" Mara asked as she opened a pack of slim cigarettes. "What luck. This is my brand."

Silence. Her host lay blank upon the hardwood flooring, bleeding from a knife wound to the gut; the blooming red was as fair as one of Rowena's prized roses. Mara marveled at her work.

"Oh, Beatrix, it's such a shame. I've ruined your pretty white blouse."

THE KILLING HOLIDAY

soundtrack

Sound and Color/Alabama Shakes

Glycerine/Bush

Goodbye Baby/Fleetwood Mac

In Too Deep/Genesis

Voices Carry/'Til Tuesday

Just Like Heaven/The Cure

Give Me The Sky/Fightstar

When You're Gone/The Cranberries

Little Girl Blue/Janis Joplin

Santeria/Sublime

Smooth Operator/Sade

Der Kommissar/After The Fire

Hungry Heart/Bruce Springsteen

Army of Me/Björk

ABOUT THE AUTHOR

Kindra M. Austin, former lunch lady and obscure internet radio show personality, is a dark fiction author and poet. Austin has one gothic horror novel (The Black Naught), one novella (The Killing Holiday), and five poetry collections (Constant Muses, TWELVE, All the Beginnings of Everything, Heavy Mental, and I Am a War) to her name.

She co-founded the feminist micro-press, Indie Blu(e) Publishing, in 2018. In her spare time, she is a LIVE reader and performer on @the.poetry.shitshow on Instagram with partner in crime, Rhiannon Marie. She is an advocate for mental health awareness, and a strong ally for the LGBTQ+ community.

Austin resides in the village of Chesaning, Michigan with her husband and their reformed feral cat. Her daughter, the source of all her inspiration, lives nearby. She loves old headstones, classic rock t-shirts from the eighties, and Norman Reedus. If you don't know who Reedus is, she feels sorry for you.

Follow Kindra M. Austin on Instagram: @kindra_m_austin

Visit Indie Blu(e) Publishing at www.indieblu.net

Indie Blu(e) Publishing is a progressive, feminist micro-press, committed to producing honest and thought-provoking works. Our anthologies are meant to celebrate diversity and raise awareness. The editors all passionately advocate for human rights; mental health awareness; chronic illness awareness; sexual abuse survivors; and LGBTQ+ equality. It is our mission, and a great honor, to provide platforms for those voices that are stifled and stigmatized.